Tabitha laid a gentle hand on Morgan's shoulder.

It was only supposed to be a show of comfort. But then he looked over at her, and as his eyes met hers, a quiver of attraction grew deep in her soul.

She didn't want to break the connection. In fact, she wanted to put her other hand on his other shoulder, like she used to. Tease him. Like she used to.

Her breath caught and it wasn't until they were jostled by someone wanting to get past them that the moment was over.

He looked momentarily taken aback as he broke her hold. Then he strode away.

Tabitha struggled with the confusion of her emotions. What was she doing? She had to stay in charge. It wasn't fair to Morgan.

She'd had her chance with him and she'd made her choice.

What if you told him what actually happened and why?

She held that thought as she made her way out the door.

Morgan was gone, and Tabitha knew there was no way she would be able to tell him what really happened. She was on her own.

Carolyne Aarsen and her husband, Richard, live on a small ranch in northern Alberta, where they have raised four children and numerous foster children and are still raising cattle. Carolyne crafts her stories in an office with a large west-facing window, through which she can watch the changing seasons while struggling to make her words obey. Visit her website at carolyneaarsen.com.

Books by Carolyne Aarsen

Love Inspired

Cowboys of Cedar Ridge

Courting the Cowboy
Second-Chance Cowboy

Big Sky Cowboys

Wrangling the Cowboy's Heart
Trusting the Cowboy
The Cowboy's Christmas Baby

Lone Star Cowboy League

A Family for the Soldier

Refuge Ranch

Her Cowboy Hero
Reunited with the Cowboy
The Cowboy's Homecoming

Hearts of Hartley Creek

A Father's Promise
Unexpected Father
A Father in the Making

Visit the Author Profile page at Harlequin.com for more titles.

Second-Chance Cowboy

Carolyne Aarsen

Recycling programs
for this product may
not exist in your area.

LOVE INSPIRED BOOKS

ISBN-13: 978-0-373-62280-1

Second-Chance Cowboy

Copyright © 2017 by Carolyne Aarsen

www.Harlequin.com

Printed in U.S.A.

So don't be afraid;
you are worth more than many sparrows.
—*Matthew* 10:31

To my nieces Amber and Chelsey who inspire me with their loving devotion to their parents.

And with thanks to my nephew Daniel Aarsen who helped me with the vet stuff.

Family is everything!

Chapter One

She was late for work. And not a *sorry I'm late* apology she could toss off while breezing into the café, flashing a contrite smile to her boss as the clock showed a few minutes past.

No, this was a serious, half an hour, *Sepp is going to fire me* late. She knew explaining to him that she was busy laying down flooring in her house until midnight wouldn't cut it. Nor would it help her case to tell him that she had to make a trip to return the nailer she had borrowed from Owen Herne.

Tabitha eased off on her truck's accelerator to make the turn, gearing down as the dust cloud following her seeped into the cab. The engine protested the sudden shift.

Please, Lord, don't let it break down, she prayed, as she shifted down again.

Her phone dinged, signaling an incoming call, then slid out of her purse and onto the floor.

Tabitha glared at the phone, then dragged her attention back to the road. No way was she hitting the ditch for the sake of a phone call.

In spite of being late, Tabitha eased off the accelerator as she turned the corner heading past the old Henry place. No one had lived in that house since Boyce and Cord Walsh bought it three years ago, but she always slowed when she drove by.

She used to dream of living there, pretending the top bedroom with its bay windows was hers and she could look out over the valley to the mountains. She had often imagined herself wandering through the many flower beds, picking lilies, daisies, lupines or lilacs to put in vases in the house. The flower beds were overgrown now, but she could still see the potential.

She preferred that dream to the reality of her place close to town. Work on the house she inherited from her father had taken up every spare moment of her time the past couple of years, and the yard was so messy and filled with junk that even thinking about it was too overwhelming.

Suddenly a large dog bounded across the road in front of her and right behind it ran a little boy.

Her foot slammed on the brakes. She wrenched on the wheel to turn the truck, her backpack falling off the seat. Her phone slid over the floor as her truck crashed into the ditch.

Her ribs hit the steering wheel with a sickening thud and her neck snapped forward. Dazed, she sat a moment, pain shooting through her ribs, radiating up her back.

She sat back, massaging her chest to make sure she hadn't broken anything. All seemed okay.

Then panic clutched her as she looked around to see what happened to the boy or the dog.

Where had they come from? She didn't know people had moved into the house.

Relief surged through her when she saw the boy

standing in the middle of the road, eyes wide, staring at her as her own heart pounded in reaction to the close call.

Then the dog jumped out of the trees and joined the boy, its tail waving joyfully as he ran in a circle around him.

Okay. Boy was fine. Dog was fine.

Tabitha took a few seconds to gather herself, then got out, pain stabbing her chest as she did.

"You okay?" she called out to the kid.

"Yeah," he said, his voice a feeble sound that showed her how afraid he was.

Then the door of the house opened and a man charged out.

"Nathan. What are you doing on the road?" he called, sounding panicked.

Then Tabitha's heart pounded in earnest as she recognized the man dropping to his knees in front of the little boy, running his hands over his face, his shoulders.

Morgan Walsh.

Her ex-fiancé, and the man who still held a large portion of her heart.

As soon as Dr. Waters told her Morgan would be working at the vet clinic, where Tabitha worked part-time as well, she had prepared herself. Had a speech all figured out.

Nice to see you. Hope you enjoy working here.

She'd even decided how she'd look. She'd be wearing her lab coat, making her look all professional and educated, her hair pulled back in a tight ponytail, her makeup perfectly done.

But at the last minute she had chickened out, telling Dr. Waters that she needed the morning off. Truth was she needed a couple more days to adjust to the idea of working with her ex-fiancé.

Morgan was part of her most painful memories. Walking away from him all those years ago was the hardest thing she had ever done. But she had broken up with him for his sake. Now here he was. A veterinarian.

So the sacrifice was worth it. And though she knew she would come face-to-face with him sometime soon, she hadn't figured on it being like this.

With her at the wheel of a truck in the ditch, her hair a tumbled disaster, her ribs aching with every quickened breath.

She gathered her wits, bending over to pick up her phone that, of course, started ringing again. She glanced at the call display. Her sister.

Tabitha tucked it in her pocket, letting it ring as she gingerly made her way through the thick grass of the ditch around the back of the truck, grimacing in pain.

Taking another deep breath, she lifted her chin and walked over to where Morgan still knelt by his son, talking to him.

"You sure you're okay?" Morgan asked again, his hands resting on the boy's thin shoulders.

"I'm fine." The boy wasn't looking at Morgan; instead he was watching Tabitha as she joined them.

Yeah, I know. I probably look like the bad side of a train wreck, she thought, delicately testing her cheekbone to see if there was any blood.

Then Morgan sensed her presence and turned, his hand resting on his son's shoulder in a protective motion. Stubble shaded his cheeks. His brown hair, as thick as ever, curled over his forehead. His blue T-shirt stretched over broad shoulders tucked into blue jeans hanging low on his hips.

He still wore cowboy boots, but the deep furrow between his eyebrows was new as was the length of his hair. He used to wear it military short. But now it hung over his collar.

He had grown more handsome over time, and in spite of her steady self-talk, Tabitha's heart twisted at the sight of his familiar, and once-loved, face.

She knew the second he recognized her. His steel-gray eyes grew cold as ice and he clenched his jaw.

"Hey, Tabitha." His voice was curt. Harsh.

The anger in his expression hurt her more than she thought it could.

"Hey, Morgan." She didn't add "good to see you" because it wasn't that good to see him.

"You almost hit my son."

He ground out the words, his voice gruff. Well, nothing like getting directly to the point, which shouldn't surprise her. She knew seeing him again wouldn't be a happy reunion of old high school friends.

The last time she'd talked to him was on the phone when she told him she was breaking up with him. He'd asked for a reason. All she would tell him was that she was over him, even as her heart and soul cried out a protest at the lies she spun.

Sure, their relationship had been a high school romance, but their feelings for each other had been deep and strong enough that they'd made plans for their wedding.

But on that horrible day she had to push all that aside. Had to prove to him that she wasn't the girl for him and that she had changed her mind about the two of them.

He tried reasoning with her but she wouldn't budge. And she couldn't tell him why. It was for his sake, she had told herself. She was doing it for him.

Then packed up and left town.

They hadn't spoken to or seen each other since.

Tabitha's phone rang again. She pulled it out and hit Decline. She'd have to call Leanne once she got to town to find out what her sister needed so badly.

"Were you talking on your phone while you were driving?" His words held the sting of accusation.

Tabitha shook her head. Mistake. Her cheek throbbed and she lifted her hand to touch it. It felt warm. It was probably already changing color.

"No." She left it at that. She'd learned too many times in her life that the more she talked, the more trouble she got into.

Case in point: Morgan's mother, who had been her high school teacher and who thought Tabitha was an unsuitable match for her vet-school-headed son. Who had warned lowly Tabitha Rennie, high school dropout, away from Morgan Walsh. He was too good for her, Mrs. Walsh had told her, and Tabitha knew it was true.

Tabitha held Morgan's gaze, then shifted her scrutiny to his son, who watched her with interest.

"You sure you're okay?" she asked Nathan.

He nodded, staring at her as if trying to figure out who she was.

"Good. And your dog is okay?"

Nathan nodded.

"Also good. Glad we don't have to bring you to the hospital or the dog to the vet. Though your dad is a vet, so maybe he could fix it himself. I usually work at the vet clinic, but not today." She caught herself, blaming her chatter on nerves. She was tempted to ask Morgan why he hadn't started work today, like she had been told, but figured that was none of her business.

So she gave the boy a semblance of a smile, then took a step back.

"Do you need a hand getting your truck out?" he asked.

Frankly, given his attitude toward her, she was surprised he offered. But country manners always took precedence over personal feelings when you lived in the ranching country of Southern Alberta. Houses were far apart and people depended on each other for help.

"No. I should be okay," she said with more bravado than she felt.

She got into her truck and waited until Morgan and his son walked away from the road, but they didn't go directly into the house. Instead Morgan stayed by the driveway, watching.

Please, Lord, let me get out of here in one go.

Then she twisted the key in the ignition.

Her truck wasn't its usual temperamental self and the engine turned over only twice before it caught.

She prayed the whole time she had her foot on the gas, her back tires spinning, tossing mud onto the road and spitting it out beside her. Her pride was on the line and she could use a win.

Finally, her tires caught the gravel, spun again, and then with a lurch she was out. She slammed on the brakes and the truck rocked to a halt.

Thanks for that, Lord, she prayed, feeling foolish that she wasted the Lord's time with such trivial things.

But it was important to her to not look bad in front of Morgan. A man who once held her heart. A man she had been forced to toss aside.

She put the truck into first gear and drove past Morgan and his son at a sedate speed.

Both of them were still watching her. One with interest, the other with a frown.

Life had just become much more complicated, Tabitha thought as she stepped on the gas and shifted into second. Hopefully she wouldn't lose her job at the café.

Again.

So, that was over and done with.

Morgan watched as Tabitha's truck drove down the road, a plume of dust roiling in its wake. Since he decided to come back to Cedar Ridge, he knew meeting Tabitha was inevitable. When Dr. Waters told him that Tabitha worked as a vet assistant in the clinic some mornings, he had almost not taken the job.

It was only when he heard she was planning on selling her place and moving eventually that he agreed. He would only have to put up with her for a short while.

"Why were you so mad at that lady?" Nathan asked, watching Tabitha leave as well.

"I wasn't mad," he said, his voice quiet, controlled as he fought down a beat of disgust at his reaction to Tabitha. Since she broke up with him all those years ago, leaving him with an engagement ring and a broken heart, he had moved on. He'd got married to Gillian. Got a degree and a son, whom his wife had kept away from him.

Three weeks ago he buried his wife and got custody of his estranged son.

A lot of changes in his life that had taken up a lot of emotions.

Yet all it took was one glimpse into those aquamarine eyes, one flip of Tabitha's copper-colored hair, one crooked smile from those soft lips for the old flame to reignite.

He had to keep his guard up if they would be working together at the clinic.

"I was scared for you," he said to Nathan, giving him a lopsided smile. "You shouldn't go running out into the road like that."

"I thought Brandy would get run over." Nathan glanced around, looking for the dog that had disappeared again. "Where did she go?"

As if on cue the dog reappeared, bounding over to Nathan, jumping around him, tongue out, tail wagging with glee.

Nathan tried to pet her but the golden retriever wouldn't stand still. His grandmother had given Brandy to Nathan as a puppy but the dog had never been properly disciplined.

Which had made the long drive here from Arizona, where Nathan's grandmother lived, even more tedious.

"That lady sure was pretty," Nathan said in a matter-of-fact voice as he picked up a stick for Brandy to fetch.

"Yeah. She was." That much he could admit.

He had a ton of things to do and to occupy his mind. Getting his son settled in and dealing with the new complication his mother-in-law had thrown at him this morning.

Gillian's mother, Donna, couldn't keep Gillian's other horse, the one she was training when she died, at her place. Could Morgan please help her out?

He would have preferred that Donna simply sell the horse, but when she asked to talk to Nathan, she'd told him about his mother's horse. And suddenly Nathan insisted that Stormy come to live with them at the ranch.

Now he had to find a way to make that happen.

"So should we start unpacking the boxes we put in your room?" he asked.

Nathan tossed the stick and Brandy took off after it. "I guess so," he said, his voice holding little enthusiasm.

"We can finish decorating your room if you want," Morgan said with a hopeful tone. "Hang up some pictures."

This got him a lackadaisical nod as Nathan watched Brandy return.

"Drop it, Brandy," Nathan commanded, but the dog wouldn't relinquish the stick.

"I think we should tie Brandy up again while we unpack," he suggested as he caught the dog by the collar. The dog immediately sat down.

"She doesn't like being tied up," Nathan protested. In fact, he had untied her a few moments ago, which was the cause of Brandy's sudden flight across the road.

"Probably not, but until she gets used to this place, it might be a good idea. You don't want her to get run over." Brandy tugged at Morgan's restraint, but he was used to handling uncooperative dogs and kept a steady pressure on the collar. "Sit," he said, and once again, she did as she was told.

"Can I untie her when I'm done?"

"If you make sure you stay in the yard with her."

Nathan stared at the dog and heaved out a long-suffering sigh. "My mom never made me tie her up."

This didn't surprise Morgan. Gillian had always prided herself on being free-spirited.

Which was probably why she never told Morgan that Nathan was his son until the boy was two years old.

"I know, but we live on a road and we don't want anything to happen to her." Morgan kept his tone even as he told Brandy to heel and led her back to the rope attached to the veranda and tied her up.

Nathan didn't reply but followed Morgan into the house. He trudged up the stairs behind him, his foot-falls heavy. Morgan knew he shouldn't expect more enthusiasm from the boy over the situation. Thanks to Gillian, the kid barely knew him.

Morgan and Gillian had met during his first year of vet school. She was in town to compete in a rodeo. They fell hard for each other, got married quickly, and then, after a year, she left him, claiming that she didn't want to be tied down.

Gillian moved back to her mother's place in Idaho and returned to the life she'd lived when she and Morgan had met. Driving around the country, pulling her horse trailer behind her, entering any rodeo she could.

Two years after she left Morgan, he found out, via her mother, that he and Gillian had a son. A five-year-long battle for visitation rights followed soon after.

For some reason, Gillian kept Nathan away from him with her constant movement, chasing her dream of being a champion barrel racer. Gillian's mother had no expla-nation either since she had become as estranged from her daughter and grandson as he was.

Then, this spring, as Gillian was competing in a rodeo up in Grande Prairie, her horse's feet went out from under him around the second barrel. Gillian fell beneath him and, in a freak accident, was crushed and in a coma. Gillian's mother, Donna, had flown in from Idaho to be at her daughter's bedside and was with her when she died hours later. Donna had also arrived with Nathan.

Thus it was at the hospital, at his wife's bedside, for the first time in the seven years Nathan had been alive, Morgan finally met his son.

They were complete strangers to each other. It was a horrible time. Nathan was withdrawn and grieving and clung to his grandmother, the only other person he was familiar with.

While Morgan was tempted to leave Nathan with Donna, he also knew the sooner he could take care of his son, the sooner they would bond.

And he also knew he needed to come back to a place where he had family and community.

Cedar Ridge.

So he contacted Dr. Waters, the local vet, about a job and managed to snag a commitment. He was supposed to start today but he'd asked if he could begin tomorrow instead.

He and Nathan had moved back to Cedar Ridge only yesterday and were barely unpacked. He wanted to spend one more day with Nathan before he went to school. Though it would be a scant three weeks before school was out, Morgan wanted to get Nathan used to the kids he would be attending school with. That way September wouldn't be as much of a shock.

Thankfully Morgan's father lived in Cedar Ridge and was willing to let Nathan come to his place after school. Cord and Ella, his brother and his fiancée, had also offered assistance as needed.

It was a patchwork support system but it would do for now.

He hoped by the time summer vacation began that he would have found a nanny or someone to help out.

"So, it's a good thing that Uncle Cord and Auntie Ella came to help us get the house organized yesterday," Morgan said to Nathan with forced joviality. "I'm sure you'll get to be good friends with your cousins Paul and Suzy."

"I never met them before." Nathan's tone indicated that he didn't care if he ever met them again. He flopped on his back on the bed, staring up at the ceiling as if the conversation was now over.

"But you'll get to know them better," Morgan replied, struggling once again with a sense of sorrow. Ever since he met Nathan, the boy had been prickly and angry and rejected every advance Morgan made.

He knew Nathan was grieving and confused and upset, and that it would take time. Morgan tried hard to understand but each rebuff was like a blow.

"When do I get to see Gramma again?" Nathan asked.

"In a couple of weeks." Donna had asked if Morgan would be willing to drive down to Idaho for her fiftieth birthday and he had agreed. The counselor he talked to had underlined the importance of maintaining contact with the one constant in Nathan's life. "But for now, let's see about making this room cozier." Morgan pulled out his jackknife to cut the tape on one of the few boxes of personal items Nathan had.

Nathan charged to life and yanked the box away from Morgan. "Don't touch my stuff," he cried.

"I was trying to help," Morgan said.

"Don't need your help." Nathan pushed the box under his bed, grabbed the other two larger ones and pulled them closer.

Morgan was too taken aback at the fury in his son's voice to reprimand him.

"Okay. You can put what you want in the dresser. There are hangers in the closet for your other clothes. Any toys you have can go in the toy box."

"Toys are for babies" was all Nathan said, shoving his hands in his pockets as he turned away from him.

His rejection was like a hit to the stomach. Morgan waited but Nathan didn't turn around.

So he left, closing the door behind him. He leaned against the wall, dragged his hand over his face and uttered a prayer for strength and patience. He simply had to give him time.

For now, Morgan had his own unpacking to do.

He was fortunate that his father owned this house, giving Morgan a place to stay. The house had been part of a ranch that Boyce and Cord had purchased a few years ago and his father was willing to subdivide the acreage and sell it to him.

And thanks to his share of Gillian's life insurance policy and his own savings, he had a down payment to put on the place. The irony of it all hadn't escaped him. Gillian had given him more in death than she had in life.

Morgan pushed away from the wall and headed down the hall to finish setting up his bedroom. The bed, dresser and the bedside table his father and Cord had picked up at a yard sale were the only pieces of furniture in a room that looked like it could house a small family.

While he worked, Morgan listened for any sounds coming from Nathan's room.

Nothing.

He was finished putting his own clothes away when his cell phone rang. It was his father.

"So, does the place feel like home yet?" Boyce Walsh asked.

Morgan looked around the bare room and chuckled. "Let's just say I'm unpacked."

"It's a start. Do you want to go out for supper?" his father asked. "I don't feel like cooking and I'm sure you don't either. We could meet at the Brand and Grill."

He hesitated. "What about the pizza place?" He wasn't so sure he wanted to meet in the same place he knew Tabitha worked.

"I hate pizza. Ate too much of that in my bull-riding days."

Morgan had to smile. His father often used his bull-riding days as a convenient excuse.

"Isn't there another place we could go?" Morgan said.

"We could do Angelo's but it's too quiet."

"Guess it's the Brand and Grill, then."

His father was quiet as if acknowledging how difficult going there could be for him.

"May as well get it over with," Boyce said. "You're going to run into Tabitha sooner or later."

"I suppose."

"Good. I'll see you and Nathan then." His father hung up and Morgan tucked his phone into his pocket, blowing out a sigh.

He certainly hadn't figured on seeing Tabitha twice in one day.

He would see her at the clinic tomorrow as well. Maybe the more often he saw her, the quicker he would get used to seeing her around.

And the quicker he could relegate any feelings he still had for her to the past, where they belonged.

Chapter Two

There they were again.

Tabitha hung back, hiding behind the wall of the kitchen as she watched Boyce, Morgan and Morgan's son, Nathan, walk into the café.

Seriously? Twice in one day?

She rolled her eyes heavenward as if asking God what He was trying to tell her.

"You going to just stand here daydreaming?" Sepp Muraski growled at her. "We got customers and supper rush is starting."

Tabitha gave her boss a forced smile. Sepp glared back at her, his dark eyebrows pulled tight together, a few curls of brown hair slipping out from under the chef's hat he wore over his hairnet.

Some might consider him good-looking. Tabitha didn't, and she suspected that was the reason he was always so grouchy with her. She had turned him down twice and he hadn't seemed to have forgiven her.

"On it," she said, straightening her shoulders and sending up a quick prayer for strength, the right words and attitude.

She would need all that and more after her encounter with Morgan and his son this afternoon.

The Walsh men were already seated when she approached them, coffeepot in one hand, menus in the other.

"Coffee?" she asked as she set the menus down in front of them.

"I'd love a cup," Boyce said with a grin, pushing his cup her way. "Pretty quiet in here," he said, making casual conversation.

Boyce stopped in at the Brand and Grill from time to time, as did Cord, Morgan's brother, so Tabitha was accustomed to seeing Walshes around. But she still had to fight a sense of shame every time she saw Boyce. She felt like she had a huge *L* written on her forehead because of the money her father had cheated Boyce out of.

I'm working on repaying it, she reminded herself, thinking of the renovations she was doing to the house she'd inherited from her father. Each new cabinet, each piece of flooring, each lick of paint made the house more sellable, which would mean more money to give to Boyce to repay him for what her father had done.

Then she could tackle the yard, a job that seemed so daunting she avoided thinking of it most of the time.

"It will get busier," Tabitha said as she turned to Morgan. "Coffee?"

He just nodded, looking at the menu.

Okay. She could do the avoiding thing too. She glanced over at Nathan, who was looking at her. "Can I get you anything?" she asked him.

"You're the lady that almost ran over Brandy," Nathan said, his tone faintly accusing.

"Not quite," she said, her ribs still sore from hitting

the steering wheel of her truck. "How is your dog?" she asked.

"She's fine." Nathan just held her gaze. "I got the dog from my gramma and soon I'm getting a horse too." His eyes brightened for a moment.

That was some generous gramma, Tabitha thought.

"What horse is this?" Boyce asked as Tabitha poured Morgan his coffee.

"Gillian's horse," Morgan put in. "She was training it before..." He paused, glancing over at Nathan.

She quickly spoke up with forced cheer. "So, Nathan, we have chocolate milk, orange juice and pop. What can I get you to drink?"

"Chocolate milk," he said, looking down at the menu again.

"Be right back." She scurried off to take care of that. She snagged a coloring book and a pack of crayons, wondering if he was too old for that, but she figured it was worth a try.

When she came back, Boyce and Morgan appeared to still be talking about the horse Nathan was expecting.

"You could get the horse trained?" Boyce said.

"But who could do it?" Morgan asked.

"My mommy was training it already." As he spoke Nathan looked more animated than he had in the past few minutes. "She loved that horse. Said it would be a real goer."

"Here's your chocolate milk," Tabitha said to Nathan. "And I thought you might enjoy this."

She set the crayons and coloring book in front of him. To her surprise, he grabbed them and opened up the book.

"Tabitha knows about horses and horse training,"

Boyce said suddenly, looking up at her. "She could help you out."

Tabitha shot him a horrified look. What was he trying to do? Surely he knew the history between her and his son?

"Would you be able to train my mom's horse?" Nathan chimed in, looking suddenly eager as he leaned past his father. "I so want to be able to ride Stormy."

Tabitha felt distinctly put on the spot. And from the glower on Morgan's face, she suspected he felt the same.

"I'm pretty busy," Tabitha said, and that wasn't too much of a stretch to say. "Two jobs, and I'm renovating the house."

"We can find someone else," Morgan said, giving his father a knowing look.

"Tabitha is capable."

"She said she was busy."

Morgan's dismissive tone shouldn't bother her. It was better for everyone if they kept their distance. Though his mother, with her relentless disapproval of Tabitha, had passed away many years ago, the shame of what her father had done to his hadn't.

When Floyd Rennie left town three years ago, he had also left a number of citizens of Cedar Ridge high and dry when he decamped with money they had invested with him for the building of a new arena. It was all part of Cedar Ridge's great hope to become part of the Milk River Rodeo Association circuit, thereby raising the profile of their local rodeo.

The arena was only half completed when her father left, taking the investors' money with him.

The most prominent of whom was Boyce Walsh. Morgan's father.

Her father died a year later, leaving Tabitha the house she was working on now. She had hoped to sell it but the real-estate agent said she could get double for it if she fixed it up.

So she began working on it in her off-hours. But it was taking much longer than she'd hoped.

"There's not many people close by who can do horse training," Boyce put in, clearly unwilling to let either Morgan or Tabitha off the hook.

"Amber could," Morgan said.

"And you know your twin sister is busy with her own life," Boyce said. "Nor is she living in Cedar Ridge."

"So, are you ready to order?" Tabitha said, pulling a pad of paper and pen out of her apron. She really needed to change the topic of conversation. Morgan clearly didn't want her around and she had no intention of spending more time with any member of the Walsh family than she needed to.

They gave her their orders and she hurried off to give them to Sepp.

"You sure were hanging around that table a long time," he grumbled. "We got other customers, you know."

She ignored him as she set up the coffeemaker to make a fresh pot of coffee. She knew well enough not to engage with Sepp.

"I don't pay you to hang around and bug the customers." He had to get one more jab in before she left.

She wished she could quit, she thought as she cleared a table, trying not to take her anger out on the hapless dishes. She wished she could walk away from Cedar Ridge. Leave it and everything it represented behind her.

But she needed the job to pay for her house renovations. She was going to finish what she had started, and she knew she couldn't leave town with her father's debt hanging over her head.

She shot a glance over at the Walsh table just as she caught Morgan looking at her. She flushed and spun away carrying the dirty dishes back to the kitchen. Adana had finally shown up and she was flirting with Sepp, who didn't seem to be in any rush to get the Walshes' orders done.

"My last order ready yet?" she asked.

"It's ready when it's ready" was all he said. "Scared I'm going to make you look bad in front of your old boyfriend?"

She knew not to say anything more. Sepp was the most passive-aggressive person she knew and the more she pushed him, the worse he would get.

A few more customers came in and Adana took their orders. Finally Sepp was done with Boyce and Morgan and Nathan's food.

"Service is getting kind of slow around here," Boyce said as she set their food on the table.

"I'm so sorry," she said, knowing she couldn't shift the blame.

"I'd say Sepp needs to hire more waitresses but I know he already has enough," Boyce continued.

Again, she could only nod as she put Nathan's burger and fries in front of him.

"Is there anything else I can get you? More coffee? Chocolate milk?"

She looked over at Nathan, who was staring at her. "Grandpa Boyce says that there's not too many people who can train horses here and that you can. Are you sure you can't?"

Were they still on that topic?

Tabitha's resolve wavered as the boy's eyes pleaded silently with her.

"Miss Rennie has other things she's busy with," Morgan said, looking at Nathan, his voice gentle. But she heard a warning in the words.

Stay away from my son.

"I'm sorry, honey," she said, giving him a look of regret. "Working here and at the clinic and fixing up my house keeps me very busy."

Then she walked away. She couldn't get involved though she felt very sorry for the little boy. She only knew snippets of the boy's story. His mother spent most of her time chasing her rodeo dreams and dragged him along. He didn't seem connected to Morgan, which made her wonder what had happened between Morgan and his wife.

Not that it mattered to her. Morgan was part of her past. She had her own plans for the future. And they didn't include sticking around a town that was such a source of pain and humiliation to her.

She couldn't afford any distractions and Morgan and his son were a huge one.

"Will you be okay?" Morgan knelt in front of Nathan on the floor of the school's hallway, handing him the backpack he had painstakingly packed this morning. Young kids ran past them, calling out to each other, their voices echoing in the busy hallway, bumping them in their rush to get to their own classes.

Yesterday morning he and Nathan had visited the school to see about enrolling him for the last few weeks of Grade Two. Though he still had his concerns, he had to think of what the counselor had told them after Gillian's death. That it was important that Morgan and Nathan find their new normal as soon as possible.

Thankfully Nathan hadn't objected to going to school, and if Morgan was honest with himself, it gave both of them a break from each other. Taking care of a seven-year-old was way out of his comfort zone. Especially a sullen young boy who rejected any advances Morgan made to him.

"This is a good school," Morgan said, injecting a bright note of enthusiasm in his voice. "I used to go here when I was a kid."

Nathan took the backpack without looking at Morgan, saying nothing.

Morgan reached out to lay his hand on his son's shoulder but Nathan pulled away, then walked into the schoolroom and went directly to his designated locker.

"You can come in with him, if you like," the perky young woman encouraged with a bright smile. "I know it's his first day here."

Just then Morgan caught Nathan looking at him, eyes wide, shaking his head a vehement "No."

Really? He couldn't even do this for his son?

He wished it didn't hurt so much.

"I think I'll stay here to see him settle in," Morgan said.

"Of course." He could tell the teacher was puzzled, but he was fairly sure she dealt with a variety of parents, so he tried not to take Nathan's clear-cut rejection to heart.

He watched a few more moments as Nathan trudged to his desk, then sat down, holding his pencil case that they had bought yesterday, looking down.

Morgan's heart broke at the sight but he felt stuck. Nathan didn't want to spend time with him, and Morgan wanted to get started at the vet clinic as soon as possible.

Wednesday, at the Brand and Grill, was the last time he'd seen Nathan act with any kind of animation when he was talking to Tabitha. Which made him nervous, especially because ever since then, the only thing Nathan would actually talk with him about was training his mother's horse so he could ride it.

And getting Tabitha to do it.

There was no way he could allow that. He didn't think he could be around Tabitha that much and, more important for his son, he didn't want him to build a connection to someone who was leaving soon.

As he drove to the clinic he found himself praying. Again. Something he'd been doing a lot lately.

Gillian's death, gaining custody of Nathan, moving back here had all taken a toll on him. Never mind working with his ex-girlfriend, whom he would be seeing again in a few minutes.

Help me to stay focused on what I need to, he prayed. *I need to be emotionally available for Nathan and protect him.*

As for his own heart, he could take care of that. The grief he had felt after Tabitha broke up with him had morphed into fury, which had settled into a dull resignation. Then Gillian came into his life and things took an entirely different twist.

His heart would be okay, he told himself. It had to be.

He checked his watch, once again thankful that Dr. Waters kept such strange hours. 9:30 seemed late to open a vet clinic but he wasn't complaining. It meant he could bring Nathan to school and still arrive on time at work. And maybe cover the occasional emergency that came up before opening hours.

He turned the corner to the vet clinic and saw Tabitha's truck parked out front.

When Dr. Waters gave him the key to the clinic yesterday, he had planned to come early. Though Dr. Waters had assured him that Tabitha, Cass and Jenny mostly manned the front desk and took care of dispensing, Morgan preferred to know where everything was himself.

He had also planned to establish his territory, so to speak, before Tabitha came in. Make the clinic his.

And now here she was already.

He sighed, sent up another prayer and headed to the back door. It was locked, so he used the key Dr. Waters had given him. He stepped inside the large open room where they worked on horses and cows. It smelled like disinfectant, and though the metal dividers for the various pens were rusted, he could see they were clean.

The rubber floor matting was also hosed down, water still trickling into the floor drain.

His footsteps echoed in the large empty space as he made his way down the concrete hallway and then through another door into the clinic proper.

He paused in the hallway, getting his bearings, then heard humming coming from one of the rooms farther down.

Tabitha, he guessed, feeling an unwelcome tightening in his chest.

He was surprised at the flicker of annoyance her obvious good mood created. Clearly she was in a good place in her life. Why that bothered him he didn't want to analyze.

She was the one who walked away from you, he reminded himself. *Of course she wouldn't pine after me.*

Like you are for her?

Not likely. She had taught him a hard lesson. He had to take care of himself and those who belonged to him.

Like Nathan.

The thought of his son was a good reminder of where his priorities now lay. And sending up another prayer for strength, he strode down the hallway.

Tabitha was working in the supply room, her hair pulled back in a loose ponytail, the early-morning sun from the window behind it creating a halo of light around her head. She was making notes on a clipboard, her lips pursed, her forehead wrinkled in a frown.

He wanted to make a joke but found himself momentarily tongue-tied, which, in turn, created a low-level frustration. Even after all these years and after all his tough self-talk, why did she still have this effect on him?

She turned around and saw him. The humming stopped as her mouth fell open and her hand clutched her chest.

"My goodness. You scared me," she gasped. "I wasn't expecting anyone this early."

"I thought..." His voice faltered and he cleared his throat. "I thought I would come in early. Get myself acquainted with the place."

"Sure. Of course. I understand." She tucked her hair behind her ear. "I'm doing some inventory."

"Okay. That's good." He wanted to say "carry on," but that would sound patronizing.

"Would you like me to show you around?" she asked, her gaze flicking from her clipboard to him.

"I guess that would be helpful."

"I can bring you up to speed on some of the animals we have staying here. Let you know what kind of work we do. In case some of it might be new to you." She stopped there, flushing.

"Sure."

She nodded and he waited, an awkward silence falling over them. "Right. I should do that now," she finally said, dropping her clipboard onto the counter in front of her. It fell and she bent over to pick it up exactly the same time he did. Their heads hit and pain jolted through him.

"Sorry," she muttered, rubbing her head just as he rubbed his.

Morgan sighed as she carefully set the clipboard on the shelf. This was getting more and more awkward. He was about to say something but she was already swishing past him, her lab coat flaring out behind her.

"The treatment rooms are here and here," she said, pointing left and right, like a flight attendant indicating escape routes, as she scurried down the hall ahead of him. "There's only two. We should have more but Dr. Waters is thrifty. Supply room you've already seen. And here's where we house the animals we've treated." Tabitha opened the door to the large back room and stepped back.

Morgan frowned as he stepped inside the dark room with its crates stacked one on top of the other.

"Looks kind of depressing." Morgan couldn't believe that there wasn't even a window or a skylight.

And it didn't smell very good.

"Do the cages get cleaned?" he asked, stopping by one of the crates, which held a Labrador pup with a plastic cone on its head. The puppy was asleep and Morgan reached between the bars and laid his hand on the dog's stomach. It was not overly warm and breathing properly.

"Of course they do. Every day."

From the defensive tone of Tabitha's voice, Morgan guessed she was the one who did the cleaning.

"The building is old and the smell tends to linger," she continued.

"Sorry. I didn't mean to imply that you're neglectful." He looked back at Tabitha, who stood in the doorway, her arms folded over her chest, her chin up, gaze challenging.

"So what's with this little guy?" he asked, pointing to the Lab.

"Hernia operation. He's due to go back today."

"And this one?" He pointed to a cat who lay on its side, one leg extended out in front of it, bandaged.

"Severed tendon on his foreleg. Got on the wrong side of a grain auger. He's lucky to be alive."

"How much small-animal work does Dr. Waters do?" Morgan glanced around the rest of the crates but they were all empty.

"Not as much as he'd like. He prefers the small animals to the large ones. I guess that's why he hired you."

Morgan nodded, remembering the conversation he and Dr. Waters had had. "And what's the large-animal patients consist of?"

"It used to be mainly cattle, but with more people moving in and more acreages sprouting up around town and people getting horses, he's doing more equine. That's my specialty but he prefers to do that on his own."

Her comment puzzled him as did the faintly bitter tone in her voice. "What do you mean, your specialty?"

"Doesn't matter. I'm just the vet assistant," she said, with a bright smile as if trying to show him she was making a joke. "We don't have specialties."

"But clearly you do," he said. He found himself suddenly curious. The last he'd heard, she had quit high school. When he found out she was working at the clinic, he had assumed it was only as a general helper.

"I went back to school a few years after I dropped out of high school. Got my high school diploma, then went to college and graduated as a veterinary assistant and equine specialist. I'm not such a dummy." She flashed a bright smile, but behind it he sensed an air of defensiveness.

"I never said you were," he returned, holding his hands up.

"Not all of us can get into vet school, but some of us can make something of ourselves."

Her tone puzzled him and he found himself wanting to ask why she'd quit school.

What he really wanted was to ask her why she'd dumped him so casually.

He pushed that last thought back into the dusty recesses of his mind. Clearly he had to do more work to let go of the past and the hurt Tabitha had caused him.

One step at a time, he told himself.

"Well, I'm glad you did. Never could figure out why you dropped out in the first place."

She looked like she was about to say something. But then the back door opened and Dr. Waters's and Jenny's voices broke into the conversation and signaled the beginning of the workday.

Tabitha spun around, striding back down the hallway, leaving Morgan confused and upset. How was he supposed to make a new start in this town when the harshest memories of his past were right here in the form of Tabitha Rennie?

Okay, Lord, You brought me here. You'll have to help me out.

His prayer was raw and rough. But it came directly from his heart. Because without God's help, he didn't think he would be able to do what he needed to do.

And that was keeping his focus on his son. He had been given a second chance with Nathan and he wasn't going to mess it up.

Not even for Tabitha.

Chapter Three

"C'mon, Tony. Since when did you need money up front from me?" Tabitha leaned on the counter, flashing a teasing grin at the young man behind the counter of Walsh's Hardware Store. "You know I'm good for it."

It was Monday morning and Tabitha had sneaked out on her coffee break to order her kitchen sink.

Morgan hadn't looked pleased at her departure, but since he'd started working at the clinic, that seemed to be his default emotion.

She knew he was stressed. Moving back home, trying to deal with a kid he barely knew. That had to be hard.

Plus, he didn't seem too happy with the fact that they had to work together. Until her house was finished, there was nothing she could do about it either.

She had kept herself busy on Saturday after working in the clinic, putting the final coat of paint on the spare room of the house, which had been her father's old room. On Sunday she stifled her guilt and put in some of the casings and baseboards, electing to stay busy and away from church. That was the trouble with a small community like Cedar Ridge. There were too many opportunities to run into people you wanted to avoid, and right now she wanted to avoid Morgan.

Besides, the sooner she got this house done, the sooner she could sell it and move on. Being around Morgan was harder than she'd thought it would be and she didn't need that extra stress in her life.

Tony nervously rearranged the ball cap he perpetually wore on his head, looking over his shoulder as if to see if the owner, George Walsh, might have made a surprise visit.

"Yeah. I know. It's just…well…your last check bounced."

"I told you why. Sepp didn't pay me on time. That's hardly my fault and I need this sink to finish the renovations on my kitchen." It had taken her a few late nights on Pinterest and home reno sites to figure out exactly which sink would fit in her kitchen. All she needed now was to order it, but Tony was being troublesome and she couldn't charm him out of it.

"I know." Tony tugged on the bill of his cap again. "Trouble is, the owner found out about the check and told my boss, Mrs. Fisher, that any more orders from you need to be prepaid."

"How did George find out?"

"He was going over the books with Mrs. Fisher and saw it. That's when he told her and she told me."

And there it was again. The ever-present Walsh influence pushing, once again, at the Rennie fecklessness.

I'm not my father, she reminded herself, stifling a far-too-familiar flush of shame. *And I'm trying desperately to fix what he broke.*

She knew it would take more than the sale of the

land and the house to make up for the thousands of dollars her father had stolen from people. But it was all she could do at this moment. And she was determined to do it right.

But if she didn't get the sink ordered, she couldn't finish her kitchen, which meant she couldn't sell the house.

Despair threatened to wash over her, and she struggled to push it back. One step at a time. And the way things were going, she wasn't sure when she could get more money. Sepp kept cutting back her hours because he claimed Adana needed them more.

She wanted to yell at him but she had no other options. Dr. Waters had made it very clear that now that Morgan was working at the clinic, the possibility of full-time work was gone.

No one seemed to need her.

"Well, I guess when you own the store, you can do what you want," Tabitha said with forced humor.

Tony shrugged.

"I'd still like to put in the order for the sink, and when I get enough together to pay for it, I'd like you to put it through," she said with more confidence than she felt.

"You don't have to pay it all," Tony said. "Just half."

Which she didn't have either.

"Just give me the total amount so I know how much I'll need." Brave talk, she thought as she gave him a cautious smile, then left. She knew exactly how much the sink, tiles and countertop would cost and how many shifts it would take her to earn that.

Too many. And now that Sepp had cut her hours back, she wasn't sure how she was going to ever catch up. Her wages at the Brand and Grill and the vet clinic covered her daily expenses. She depended heavily on her tips for the extras.

As she walked down the street to her truck, she fought down her anger at Sepp's unreasoning dislike of her, and at a father who had let her and her sister down so badly.

She checked the time and hurried her steps. She made quick work of getting to the clinic and slipping inside.

"Anything happen while I was gone?" she called out to Jenny as she pulled on her lab coat.

"Nope. Pretty quiet. Morgan went out. He got a call from the school about Nathan acting up," Jenny said as Tabitha joined her in the front office. "Asked me not to tell Dr. Waters, so I'm hoping he stays away on his call long enough for Morgan to come back." She tut-tutted her disapproval. "Dr. Waters has already made a lot of concessions for him. Only the second day on the job and already—"

She stopped talking as the front door opened and Morgan stepped inside, looking harried.

"Everything okay?" Tabitha asked.

His eyes looked at her, then looked away. "Yeah. Fine."

The curt tone in his voice told her that, clearly, everything was not fine. So did the frown on his face.

Don't engage, she told herself. *He clearly doesn't want my help.*

"You don't look fine," Jenny pressed. "Everything go okay with Nathan?"

Morgan shook his head, the look of concern on his face making Tabitha feel bad for him. "He's been having a hard time at school," he said. "I knew it would be a difficult transition for him, but he seemed excited about it at the time. He's just having trouble settling in."

"Moving to a new school is tough," Tabitha added. "I feel sorry for the little guy."

"I'm sure you would know what he's dealing with," Morgan said.

His admission and the faint smile accompanying it startled her. It was the first hint of softness she'd received from him. For a moment she longed to explain to him what had happened all those years ago, but she quashed that. It was so long ago it hardly mattered anymore. Besides, even if she did tell him, that didn't change the fact of what her father had done to his father. That couldn't be explained away. She could only fix things by staying on the course she had set for herself.

Then his cell phone rang and Morgan looked at the call display. "Sorry, gotta take this." He answered the phone as he walked away.

Jenny watched him go, then sighed. "That poor man. He's got a lot to deal with. Must be rough being a single parent. Too bad there's not some single girl for him." She looked over at Tabitha. "Actually, I heard a rumor the other day that you two used to date."

Date was hardly the word for the deep and abiding feelings she had felt for Morgan, she thought with a touch of melancholy.

They had made plans to get married. Move away from Cedar Ridge. Start a new life away from the expectations of his mother and the reputation of her father.

"That was a long time ago," Tabitha said. "It was just a high school fling."

No sooner had she spoken the words than Morgan

stepped into the room. From his expression, she guessed he had heard her.

Then the door flew open and a woman rushed in. "My cat got attacked by a dog." Tabitha recognized Selena Rodriguez, an older woman who owned the Shop Easy. She looked around, eyes wide, her long graying hair damp but pulled up in a clip.

Morgan hurried over, pulling a pair of latex gloves out of his pocket, and did a cursory exam of the cat. "I'll take him," he said and glanced over at Tabitha. Cass, the other vet assistant, had left on a job with Dr. Waters, so it was on her to help.

She knew it would happen sooner or later that she would have to work closely with Morgan, and she thought she was prepared for it.

But when she stood across from him at the exam table, their faces covered with masks with only their eyes visible, she felt a momentary discomfort. She was close enough to see the fan of wrinkles at the corner of his eyes. Smell his aftershave. He smelled different, took up space in a different way. His shoulders were broader, his hair longer.

Regret washed through her. What if she hadn't listened to his mother all those years ago? What if she'd had enough confidence in her feelings for Morgan?

But she hadn't and she didn't, and she couldn't spend her life living with regret over might-have-beens.

Then her training took over and she pushed her own emotions aside. *He's not for you. There's too much between you*, she told herself.

Then together they started an IV to anesthetize the cat, then intubated him. As they fell into a routine, and she began prepping the sites, she looked at him as just another vet stitching up some cuts on a cat.

"Looks like we got done on time." Cord dropped his hammer into the hook on his pouch as a dually pickup pulling a stock trailer roared onto the yard. "Here comes your horse."

It was Tuesday evening, and Morgan and his brother had just finished fixing up a makeshift corral to hold Gillian's horse, Stormy, until Morgan could figure out what to do with it. Cord had offered to board it at the ranch, but Nathan had protested loudly. He wanted Stormy on the yard.

So for now, he would keep it here and feed it hay. Not the best solution, but his bigger concern was for Nathan more than the horse.

"I sure hope those old posts hold," Cord said as they watched as Ernest, who drove the truck, turned and backed up to the gate.

Morgan gave his brother a look. "You were the one who assured me they would be strong enough."

Cord punched him lightly on the arm with one gloved fist. "I'm just bugging you. Relax."

"Don't know how to do that anymore," Morgan muttered, looking over at his son, who stood by the fence fairly vibrating with excitement. It was the happiest Morgan had seen him since he got here.

"How are you two getting along?" Cord questioned.

Morgan thought of the boxes the boy still hadn't unpacked. The phone calls with the teachers this afternoon. They had found Nathan in the bathroom, huddled in a stall, crying.

Morgan had been in the middle of a C-section on a

cow and couldn't come to school, and Nathan wouldn't talk to him on the phone. So Morgan had called his father, who lived in town. After Boyce picked him up, he called to tell him that everything was okay. He and Nathan were having cookies and milk, and another crisis had been averted.

"Step by step" was all he could say, something that applied to his job, it seemed, as well as to his relationship with his son. "I don't suppose you know anyone who could work as a nanny."

Cord just laughed. "I had my own struggles and then Ella came into our lives." He grinned at him. "So that's your solution. You need to find a wife."

"No, thanks. Already had one and you saw how well that worked out. Besides, Nathan is my priority and I'm having a hard enough time connecting with him."

Cord looked at the boy leaning against the fence, watching everything with interest. "Give it time. He's been through a lot and he's probably confused. Plus he's still grieving for his mother."

Morgan nodded. But there was no more time for conversation. The trailer had backed up and the truck engine turned off.

Ernest came around to the back of the trailer, hitching up his baggy pants, his eyes bright under unkempt eyebrows. "Well, she's a feisty one," he said with a grin. "Took two guys to get her haltered and loaded. Watch out for her hooves when you go inside."

"Maybe let me unload her," Cord said, holding up his hand to stop Morgan.

Morgan looked at Nathan, who was intently watching the proceedings.

"No. I need to do this," he said, yanking on the door's

latch, slipping it up and pulling open the sliding door. Nathan needed to see him leading the horse.

As soon as he stepped inside, Stormy whinnied, her eyes wide, ears pinned back, her back foot striking hard at the wall of the trailer.

"Easy, girl," Morgan said, walking slowly toward her, pushing down his own trepidation. A horse like this could be unpredictable and therefore dangerous in such a small space.

Stormy stepped back, trembling now, head up and ears still back as he came closer.

He saw Cord peering in the side of the trailer and, in spite of his concern, he had to grin. Big brother watching out for him.

"It's okay, girl. I'm going to untie you and lead you out of this trailer." He pitched his voice low. Quiet. Hoping it would settle the horse down.

He carefully untied the rope. She jerked back, the rope slipped in his hands, and then, before he knew what was happening, she landed on her front feet and hit his shoulder as she shot past him out of the trailer and into the corral.

"You okay?" he heard Cord call out.

"Yeah. I'm fine." His pride was hurt more than his shoulder.

He stepped out in time to see Stormy charging around the corral, rope trailing behind her as Cord rushed to close the gate. Appropriate name, Morgan thought, rubbing his shoulder. Before anyone could stop him, Ernest jumped over the corral fence and snagged the halter rope. Stormy pulled away, Ernest pulled back, and then the horse was suddenly still.

Nathan, unaware of what was going on, laughed,

clapping his hands at the sight as he watched through the railing.

"Looks like this horse will need some training," Cord said.

"Grandpa Boyce said that Miss Tabitha knows how to train horses," Nathan put in. "He said my dad should ask her but she said she was busy and my dad said we would find someone else."

Morgan had to stifle a beat of frustration with his father. He knew about his previous relationship with Tabitha. Why did he keep pushing?

Then Ernest joined them, leaning one elbow on the rail, tugging on his mustache. "She's a good horse. Good feet. Good conformation. She's jumpy, though."

"I want to ride her," Nathan said, watching Stormy as she now stood, her sides heaving with exertion.

"You won't be riding her for a while," Ernest warned, shaking his head. "That horse needs a firm but gentle hand and a lot of training."

"And you can't do it?" Morgan asked. Ernest had trained a number of horses. Though he hadn't for some time, Morgan thought it was worth asking.

Ernest pulled in a breath, then gave Morgan a look tinged with regret. "No. That's a young man's game and I don't have it in me anymore. Have you asked Tabitha? I helped train her. She's a natural, though she hasn't done much of it since she moved back here."

Again with Tabitha?

"Not an option" was all Morgan would say.

"Will I never be able to ride my mom's horse?" Nathan said, his chin now trembling. He looked up at Morgan, who was disconcerted by the tears in the boy's eyes.

"We'll figure something out, Nathan," Morgan said,

kneeling down and catching his son by his narrow shoulders. "Don't worry. You'll be able to ride her. Just not right away."

"So Miss Tabitha will train her?" Nathan asked, wiping his tears away with the back of one dusty hand.

"I said we'll figure something out" was all he said. Though he didn't like the way the conversation was going, at least Nathan was talking to him. That was a plus.

Nathan nodded, seemingly satisfied with this answer.

"I better clean out that trailer and get on my way," Ernest said, pushing away from the fence. "Nathan, you want to help me?"

"Sure." Nathan scooted past Morgan looking happier than he had in a while.

Morgan waited until he was out of earshot, then turned to his brother.

"So what do you think I should do?" he asked. "That horse isn't rideable and Nathan seems to think it might happen."

"A horse you can't ride is taking up space and eating valuable hay," Cord said, ever the practical rancher.

"But Nathan seems attached to the beast because it belonged to Gillian." Morgan sighed, resting his arms on the rail, watching the horse going round and round the pen. "He's the most enthusiastic when he talks about that horse. Nice change from the slightly depressed kid I usually see. But I can't find anyone to train it except, it seems, for Tabitha." He sighed again. "And I'm not sure I want to go down that road. Bad enough I have to work with her. At least at the clinic there are boundaries."

"If she is training this horse, she'll need to be working with Nathan."

Morgan sighed. "I know, but truth is, I don't think she has the time. She's working two jobs and renovating her house."

"Probably just as well." Cord held his brother's gaze as he released a hard breath. "She broke your heart once before. Word on the street is that she's only in town long enough to fix up that place her dad left to her and sell it. She'll take the money and move on, just like her dad. You've got a kid now. He's what you have to think about. Keep Tabitha in the past, where she belongs."

"I think I can handle myself with Tabitha," Morgan returned, feeling a surge of frustration that his brother seemed to think one look into those blue-green eyes would turn him into a mindless lunatic.

Cord nodded, as if he didn't believe his brother's protests.

"I'll get the rest of the fencing stuff" was all Cord said.

But as his brother walked away, Morgan pondered Cord's words. Worst of it was, even in spite of his tough talk, he knew his brother was right.

Fool me once, he thought, heading over to where his son was chatting with Ernest.

He couldn't afford to trust so blindly again.

Chapter Four

Sepp looked up from scraping the deep fryer, glowering at Tabitha as she dropped a couple of mugs by the dishwasher. "Kind of dead this afternoon." His voice was accusatory. As if it was her fault.

"For a Wednesday afternoon it sure is," Tabitha agreed, reminding herself to stay pleasant.

"You may as well go home." Sepp looked back at what he was doing. "No sense paying you to hang around if there's so few customers."

"Things might pick up," she said, trying not to sound too desperate. Any tip she might get, any dollar she made, brought her that much closer to getting her kitchen finished.

"If they haven't by now, they won't in half an hour," he snapped. She wanted to argue but she knew better than to contradict Sepp and cross him when he was in an ornery mood.

Instead she pulled off her apron and set it in the laundry bin, then took her backpack off the hook at the back of the kitchen. "I'll see you tomorrow morning, then."

Sepp stood back from the fryer. "You don't need to sound so testy."

Tabitha pulled in a slow breath, seeing the banked anger in Sepp's eyes. The past few days he'd been sniping and griping at her even more than usual.

"I'm sorry. I'm just tired." She worked on the house until late last night again, putting in the last of the casings and baseboards to finish up the bedroom.

"Tired from hanging around with Morgan Walsh?"

She tried not to roll her eyes, but as she looked at him, she realized maybe that was his problem. He was jealous of Morgan.

"Morgan is the last person I want to be with on purpose." That wasn't entirely true. She had already spent a week working with Morgan, and each time she saw him it became harder to maintain her distance.

"So, you're not seeing him?"

Tabitha blew out a sigh. "No. I'm not."

He nodded. "So then, are you free Friday night?"

Tabitha could only stare, not sure which of his questions disturbed her more. The one about Morgan or the one asking her out.

"I'm busy. I'll always be busy for you." Too late she realized that she had overstepped a boundary she kept scrupulously in place. She had always been evasive with Sepp, cautiously refusing his advances. But she had never been this rude with him.

"Okay. Well, then maybe you don't need to bother coming in for a while."

Tabitha stared at him, suddenly tired of his machinations, his threats and his borderline obsession with her. As long as she kept turning him down it would never end. He would cut her hours back and back. And she was sick of it.

"Well, I won't bother coming in at all, then. I quit." She wished she hadn't already taken her apron off. It would have given her the perfect dramatic exit. Pull off apron. Toss it aside. Turn and storm away without a backward glance.

Instead she shifted her backpack on her shoulder and strode away.

But as soon as the back door of the café slapped shut behind her, dread flooded through her. What had she just done? Quit the job that paid her the most money?

How was she supposed to pay for the rest of her house renovations now?

She leaned against the exterior of the café, the stucco digging into her skin through her shirt. Now what was she going to do?

"I'm sorry, but I'm wondering if it's in Nathan's best interests to be in school right now. It's almost the end of the school year, so he won't miss much." The Grade Two teacher, Miss Abrams, gave Morgan a gentle smile, as if to soften her words. She glanced over at Nathan, who sat hunched on the cot in the school nurse's office, his arms wrapped around his legs, staring out the window. "He's had a lot to deal with the past few months. He's a smart boy. In my opinion he might be better off to spend time with you at home."

She sounded so reasonable and Morgan could hardly fault her for her advice. But how was he supposed to do that?

Morgan looked over at Nathan, who wasn't looking at him. He wasn't crying now but had been an hour ago. Morgan had been out of cell range, working in a farmer's back field on a sow that had farrowed, and she and her newborn piglets had been attacked by a coyote.

By the time they got the sow fixed up and carted on a trailer with her piglets back to the farmer's yard, he was back in service. Then his cell phone dinged steadily with messages from the school. He tried to call his father but he wasn't around. Neither were Cord or Ella. So he told Dr. Waters he had to go to the elementary school, earning him a scowl and a slight reprimand.

He knew it didn't look good. Barely a week on the job at the vet clinic and things were falling apart for him at home. But what else could he do?

"If that's what you think should happen," Morgan said.

"I do," Miss Abrams said. "I know it's not an easy solution, but Nathan needs some time with you more than he needs school right now."

Morgan stifled another sigh. Part of him knew she was right, but he wasn't sure how this was going to work.

"I'll take him home," Morgan said. He put his hand on his son's shoulder and, to his surprise, the boy didn't flinch away. He looked up at Morgan, looking so bereft Morgan knelt and pulled him into his arms.

Nathan stayed there a moment, resting his head against Morgan's neck. His son, he thought, a rush of pure joy flowing through him.

But then Nathan pulled back, withdrawn again.

"We're going back home," Morgan told him.

"Which one?"

The question hit Morgan like a blow. He knew Gillian had moved around a lot. Had his son no sense of which place was home?

"We're going to the ranch. Where Stormy is."

His face lit up at that. "I really want to see Stormy again. I think she misses me when I'm in school."

"Maybe she does."

He picked up Nathan's backpack and held out his hand, but Nathan jumped off the cot and hurried ahead of him toward the door.

Morgan thanked Miss Abrams and, as they walked back to the truck, Nathan smiled. "I'm excited to ride my mom's horse," he said, looking ahead as if imagining himself doing so.

"I'm sure you are," Morgan said. The school counselor he had spoken to before he picked Nathan up had mentioned that the only time Nathan seemed to show any life was when he talked about his mother's horse. She suggested that Morgan let Nathan fantasize about the horse and riding it. Affirming his comments, she said. Morgan wasn't entirely sure how to go about that, so he figured he would treat Nathan's suggestions like he had his twin sister Amber's when they were growing up. Agree and nod and smile.

"But I can't until Stormy is trained," Nathan said.

"That's true."

Nathan said nothing. Instead he stared out the window.

"I have to stop by at the clinic for a minute," Morgan said. He had forgotten to write down the billable hours for the call he did this morning.

Nathan just nodded. At least he wasn't crying.

Morgan pulled up to the clinic, dismayed to see

Tabitha's truck parked there. What was she doing back here? He thought she worked at the café in the afternoon.

"Isn't that the truck of the lady who almost ran over Brandy?" Nathan asked.

"Yes. It is," Morgan said.

"Her name is Miss Tabitha, isn't it? And she works at the café? She gave me a coloring book and crayons even though I'm not a little boy. But it was nice. And Grandpa Boyce says she's the lady that trains horses."

"Yes. Miss Tabitha does train horses," Morgan answered. "But she's very busy working for Dr. Waters and Mr. Sepp at the café." Morgan hoped he got the hint as he helped him out of the truck.

Nathan walked ahead of Morgan, skipping a little, looking a lot happier than he had in a while. Guess sending him to school hadn't been such a good idea after all. Guess he wasn't much of a father for not knowing that.

Morgan opened the door and, as always, his eyes had to adjust from the bright summer sun to the windowless back room with its pens and gates. He wondered why Dr. Waters hadn't at least put a skylight in here. Or replaced some of the penning. One of these days some animal was going to lose it in here and bust one of the rusted posts.

"Wow. What do you do here?" Nathan asked.

"This is where we work with cows and horses and bigger animals like that."

Nathan nodded as he followed Morgan through another door and down the hall to the front office, checking out the posters of dogs and cats and various other animals lining the walls between rooms.

In the office, Tabitha stood by the desk, talking to

Jenny, her one hand pressed to her cheek, her other clutching her elbow. She looked like she'd been crying.

"I doubt Dr. Waters will give you more hours," Jenny was saying.

"Why should he? He barely gives Morgan enough. Dr. Waters is running around like a fool himself, losing business because he can't keep up. Makes me wonder why he hired Morgan in the first place."

"Are you kidding? Who in Cedar Ridge would ever say no to a Walsh?"

"And who would say yes to a Rennie? We both know what my father's reputation has done for my sister and me. Now that I quit the café, how am I ever going to pay off my bills and finish that wretched house? And I still have a ton of cleaning up to do." She stifled another sob, pressing her hand to her mouth.

Morgan held back, realizing he had stumbled into a very personal but potentially disturbing conversation. He gathered that Tabitha had lost her job at the café. But what surprised him more was his reaction to her tears. He wanted to rush into the room and pull her into his arms. Comfort her like he used to whenever she was upset.

He was about to back away and wait until those impulses passed, but Nathan had finally caught up to him. He saw Tabitha and went running past Morgan into the room.

"Hi! You're Miss Tabitha, aren't you?" he said, smiling up at her.

Tabitha's reddened eyes grew wide as she looked from him to Morgan, who now stood in the doorway. She spun away, swiping at her face.

Morgan shot a warning frown at Jenny, who wasn't

looking at him either. He guessed she wasn't too proud of her "he's a Walsh" comment.

Nor should she be. Morgan liked to think that his high GPA, his stellar reputation at his previous vet clinic and his strict work ethic had been the reason Dr. Waters hired him.

Not his last name.

"Why is Miss Tabitha crying?" Nathan said, turning to Morgan. "Why is she sad?"

"I'm okay." Tabitha sniffed, then turned back to Nathan.

"I was crying too," Nathan said, looking back at Tabitha. "I miss my mommy and I want to ride her horse but I can't."

Tabitha gave him a wavery smile and touched his head lightly. "I'm sorry you can't." Then she looked puzzled. "And why aren't you in school?"

He shrugged, suddenly very interested in the hem of his worn T-shirt. "School makes me sad," he said, twisting it around his hand. He managed to poke a hole in it and wiggled his finger through it, making it bigger. "So my daddy says I don't have to go anymore."

"But who will take care of you?" Tabitha glanced over at Morgan, who simply shrugged. He wished he knew too.

Just then Cass came into the office and dropped a file on the desk. She looked around. "Am I missing something?"

Jenny stood and nodded at the other vet assistant. "Why don't you take Nathan to see the new puppy we're taking care of?"

Cass frowned, and then Jenny raised her eyebrows,

motioned her head down the hall, and suddenly Cass seemed to get whatever hint Jenny seemed to be giving.

"Nathan. Do you want to see an adorable Labra-doodle puppy?" Cass said, sounding puzzled but obviously going along with whatever Jenny seemed to be planning.

Nathan grinned. "Labradoodle. That's a funny name." But he willingly trotted along behind Cass.

"So. Tabitha just lost her job at the café." Jenny turned to Morgan. "And now you have your son, who can't go to school and who, in my opinion, probably shouldn't have been going to school. The other day you were asking me for names of a nanny and Tabitha was asking me if there's anyplace that's hiring. Seems to me we have a solution to two problems in one right here."

"Wait a minute—"

"But—"

Both Morgan and Tabitha spoke at once. Jenny held up her hand. "Do you have a nanny for your son? Do you know of anyone who can do it for you? I know you're willing to pay decent money because you told me so."

He realized the sad truth of what she was saying. "No. I don't." He felt like a kid being quizzed in school and sensed where Jenny was going. But he wasn't going to be the first to say anything. Ten years ago Tabitha had roundly rejected him. He wasn't about to allow her to do it again on purpose.

"Tabitha, you just came back from walking around town trying to find a job. With no success." She held one hand out to her and the other out to Morgan. "Morgan here needs a nanny. You need a job." Jenny wove her fingers together, indicating a perfect fit. "Voilà. Both problems solved."

Morgan could see Tabitha was fighting her own reaction to the situation. He wished it didn't bother him that she was so reluctant to help. But at the same time, he knew he was being hypocritical. He wasn't keen on her spending time with his son either.

She glanced over at him, her eyebrows lifted in a question. "What do you think? Do you trust me to take care of your son?"

"Guess I have to," he said.

He knew he could sound more gracious than that, but Jenny was right.

He didn't have a choice.

Chapter Five

"Have you seen my mom's horse?" Nathan asked Tabitha after he was done with his lunch. He was sitting at the kitchen island, head propped in his hands, elbows resting on the high counter as he watched Tabitha clean up the kitchen.

Tabitha had arrived at the house early this morning determined to create a good impression. Morgan was also ready to go and he had given her cursory instructions. It wasn't hard to tell that he was still reluctant to have her in his house, yet they both knew Jenny had been right.

They needed each other.

"No, I haven't," she said, tidying up the papers spread out over the dining room table. She and Nathan had spent the morning going over the assignments the school had emailed to Morgan and that he had printed out. Her heart had sunk when Morgan had informed her that he hoped she would help Nathan with his schoolwork. Just to keep him up to speed.

Tabitha had reluctantly agreed. Thankfully he was only in second grade and she had managed to get him to read all his assignments aloud to her as they worked through them.

Nathan didn't seem to notice any hesitancy on her part. He seemed happy enough to be at home instead of school.

Now he was bouncing his head in time to the country music Tabitha played on the radio in the kitchen, ketchup from the macaroni she had made him streaked on one cheek, his long hair sticking up. He needed a haircut but there was no way she was taking care of that. Morgan seemed hesitant enough to have her watch Nathan. She got it, she really did. Because she felt the same reluctance and it only grew with each minute she spent with Nathan. Being around him all morning had created an unwelcome pang of sorrow. Made her wonder what kind of children she and Morgan would have had.

"I haven't," Tabitha said again, taking his plate from him.

"Can we go see her now? I'm done with all my work."

"Is she here?"

"Mr. Ernest brought her here on Tuesday." He grinned, swiping his sleeve over his mouth, moving the ketchup smear to his shirt. Tabitha made a paper towel wet and walked around the island.

"We can go see her, but first let me wipe the ketchup off your shirt," she said.

He held out his arm and she cleaned it as best as she could. The shirt was worn and thin. So were his pants. Tabitha wondered again why Morgan hadn't purchased any new clothes for him.

She looked around the house again at the sparse furnishings of the spacious, open-plan home. A large leather sectional and a television on a wooden shelf were all that filled the living room. An old worn table and four folding chairs huddled around it in the dining area.

Nothing hung on the walls. There were no curtains at the window. It broke her heart. She had imagined the interior of this home so many times, but never in all her dreams did it look this bare and unwelcoming.

She knew Morgan wasn't short of cash. When he told her what he was willing to pay her, she was surprised. Pleased, but surprised. And she'd had to swallow her pride and thank him for it.

All for the cause, she reminded herself.

"Can you wipe my cheek too?" Nathan asked, holding his face up to her. "I think I have ketchup on it too."

She cupped his chin in her hand and gently wiped the remnants of the smear off his cheek. The smile he gave her created another tremor of sorrow at the thought of might-have-beens with Morgan.

She pulled back with a start. She couldn't let this little guy into her heart.

"Let's go see your horse," she said. Nathan jumped off his chair and ran out the door, leading the way.

She followed him across the cracked sidewalk then down a worn gravel path to the corral. Brandy the dog had jumped up from her place in the sunshine and followed them, her tail waving. Nathan ran ahead, the dog at his heels, and Tabitha smiled at the sight. Life distilled to its essence, she thought, watching as Nathan stopped and petted Brandy, then hurried on.

A large bale of hay with a fork stuck in it sat by the corral where a gray horse stood, head over the fence, looking expectant.

"She's always hungry," Nathan said, walking over

to her. But the horse shied away when he came near. "And I don't think she likes me."

"She doesn't know you yet, that's all," Tabitha said, coming closer to the fence. She leaned her arms on the top rail, warmed by the sun. A delicate summer breeze rustled the leaves of the trees surrounding the corral and teased her hair away from her face. Between working at the veterinary clinic and her job at the café and renovations on the house in the few hours she could carve out, she didn't get to spend much time outdoors. "What's her name?"

"Stormy," Nathan said. "Morgan said I can't ride her yet."

"This is the horse you wanted me to train?" she asked, watching as Stormy trotted around the corral, head up, eyes wide.

"Yes." Nathan grabbed her arm. "You're here now. Why don't you train her?"

"I haven't gotten permission from your father to do that." He hadn't seemed crazy about the idea of her training the horse before.

"But you're here now."

"I know." And if she was honest, the horse made her curious. She had trained horses with Ernest, and each time a new horse came on his yard, she felt a tiny rush of energy. What would this horse be like to work with? What was its personality? Its strengths and weaknesses?

She felt the same questions now as she watched Stormy striding back and forth. She had a lovely gait and would make an excellent riding horse.

"But she's my mom's horse, not my dad's…not Morgan's." His voice took on a petulant tone but Tabitha caught the faint hesitation before he spoke Morgan's name.

"Why don't you call Morgan Dad?" she asked.

Nathan looked down, his mouth forming a hard line. "My mom said he wasn't a good dad. He didn't keep his promises."

She wanted to ask but part of her felt a need to keep a distance.

Don't get involved. You can't fix this.

It broke her heart but she knew she had to maintain some emotional distance. This time she was determined to leave Cedar Ridge with her heart whole. She couldn't do that if she got too close.

"I can have a look at her, I guess," Tabitha said, climbing over the fence, watching her to see how Stormy would react. The horse immediately jumped to one side, trembling as she stood.

She turned to the dog, who sat beside Nathan. "Brandy, you stay." The dog looked at her, then lay down. "Make sure that the dog doesn't come into the pen, okay?" she said to Nathan.

He nodded and squatted down beside Brandy, holding her by the collar. Tabitha waited but it looked like the dog understood her command.

Tabitha turned back to Stormy as she walked to one side of the pen, her eyes on the horse, keeping her distance for now. Stormy shied again. Tabitha spent a few minutes observing and she could see the horse relax.

She waved her arms and Stormy ran to one corner, but Tabitha kept pushing her and Stormy started moving. Tabitha had never worked with a horse in a square pen before and was unsure, but when Stormy moved into the corner, Tabitha waved her arms at her again and thankfully Stormy kept moving.

"Why are you scaring her?" Nathan called out.

"This is what horses do in a herd," she said, keeping the horse going, wishing she had a stick to wave around as well to help guide her. "They chase the horse away so the horse understands who's in charge, and that's what I'm doing here." She kept the horse moving, watching for cues that the horse was ready to "talk" to her. "See, when horses are in a herd they have to work together, but to work together, they have to listen and obey the boss horse. Stormy needs to know I'm the boss."

"But don't you want her to be your friend?" Nathan asked, sounding concerned.

Tabitha chuckled at that. "See, that's the difference between Brandy and Stormy. Brandy is looking for a friend. Stormy is looking for a leader. Two different animals, two different things."

Stormy went around a few more times and Tabitha felt distracted, watching to make sure Nathan and Brandy stayed, that the horse didn't push the fence, and yet keeping up her momentum.

But Nathan seemed content to stay beside his dog. Then, after a few more go-rounds, Tabitha saw Stormy slow, drop her head and start the chewing motion that signaled her willingness to now "talk" to Tabitha.

Tabitha stopped in the middle of the pen and Stormy turned to her. Perfect. Just what she wanted. Tabitha waited where she was, talking to Stormy, and then, to her surprise, the horse walked directly to her. Tabitha reached out and laid her hand on Stormy's neck. She felt a tiny tremor, a little rejection, but Stormy stayed where she was. Clearly someone had done some work with her already.

"Good girl," Tabitha cooed, slipping her hand over her neck, then down her back. "Good girl."

She turned to show Nathan, and her heart jumped. Morgan was walking down the trail toward the pen. And he didn't look pleased.

"Tabitha, what are you doing?" Morgan kept his voice low when he saw that Tabitha was looking at him.

"Working with Stormy." She held her chin up, holding his gaze, but she sounded defensive.

He was about to ask her if she knew what she was doing, but with that crazy horse standing quietly beside her as Tabitha turned back to her, stroking her, the question was useless.

Clearly she did.

After Cord and Ernest had dropped Stormy off, the horse had kicked at the fence, bared her teeth at Morgan when he tried to come close and, in general, acted like a horse who was asking for a one-way ticket to the auction market.

It was because Nathan saw this horse as a tangible connection to his mother that Morgan knew he would never get rid of the animal.

"Well, I'm impressed," he said.

His words seemed to surprise her. He suspected she assumed he would say something entirely different. And he might have but for the evidence in front of him.

"This is only a small step," she said. "But an important one."

"Do you think she's trainable?" Morgan asked, glancing down at Nathan. But his son's eyes were fixed on Tabitha and Stormy and didn't even look at him.

His rejection, as it always did, cut him deeply.

"I believe she is," Tabitha said. "She's a beautiful animal with a lot of potential."

Nathan jumped up and, to Morgan's surprise, grabbed his hand, getting his attention. "I want Miss Tabitha to train Stormy so I can ride my mom's horse."

He looked down at Nathan and curled his fingers around his hand, thankful for this tiny connection. As he held Nathan's pleading gaze, he knew he couldn't say no. Initially he'd had his concerns about Tabitha training Stormy because it would mean her spending more time with Nathan.

Well, that was a moot point now that she was taking care of him.

"Do you think you can get her close to rideable before you leave?" he asked, flicking his gaze to her.

Tabitha looked back at Stormy, whom she was still petting, then back at him and gave him a curt nod. "I can make her rideable for an adult. But before a kid can mount her, we're looking at time and miles by an adult."

"I can take care of that," he said. He'd spent enough time on the back of a horse to know what was required.

"Then I can do this." She petted the horse, looking around at his yard. "There is one problem, though. This corral doesn't look very strong and I'm wondering about pasture."

He was well aware of both problems. "This was strictly temporary," he said. "Until I could find someone to train her."

"Well, now you have. But I was wondering if you would be willing to move her to my place. I can work with her better there in my round pen, and I have a decent fenced-in pasture."

"But I won't be able to see her if you take Stormy to your place," Nathan cried out.

"I could take Nathan with me in the afternoons I'm working with him," Tabitha suggested.

"Yay! That would be so cool," Nathan said, still clinging to Morgan's hand. "Can we do that? I really want to go to Miss Tabitha's place."

"You've never been there," Morgan said with a gentle smile.

"But I think it would be cool. And Miss Tabitha is fun to be with."

Morgan knew he didn't have a lot of choice. Nathan's life had already been tossed around enough and he seemed to have formed an attachment to Tabitha.

Which was exactly what he was afraid would happen.

He looked over at Tabitha, surprised to see a tender smile on her face as she looked from him to Nathan. Then Brandy jumped up, barking at who knew what as she ran toward the house, and Nathan ran to follow her.

Tabitha petted the horse one more time then walked to where Morgan stood. "I understand your concerns," she said. "I know you're scared he'll connect with me and I'll leave him in the lurch when I leave. I get that. But I promise you I'll be careful with him. I won't hurt him."

Morgan held her earnest gaze, and in spite of what had happened and what she had done, he felt a softening of the barrier he had placed around his heart.

Her green eyes, the way the sun shone on her copper hair, making it glint like a precious coin, brought back memories of happier times. For a moment they were younger, breathless, blissfully happy simply being together.

"I'd like to believe you." He meant to speak the words

in anger. Push her away. But to his disappointment they came out like a request.

"You can," she said, a shadow of pain flitting across her features. "I know you have every reason not to trust me, but on this you can believe me. I'll be careful with your son."

He held her gaze a split second longer than he should. Allowed himself a moment of remembrance, and then he pulled back and nodded. "Okay. I believe you."

"Thanks." She released a shaky breath that made him wonder if she was as unsettled around him as he was around her. "So now we need to make arrangements to move Stormy to my place," she said.

"I'll give Ernest a call. See if he can do it sometime this week."

Tabitha looked back at Stormy, who still stood, watching, as if gauging what she was up against. Then Tabitha climbed over the fence. Morgan had to clench his fists to stop himself from helping her over. Given his current state of mind, he was afraid he would hold on to her too long.

But she was up and over and walking ahead of him before he could give in to the temptation. "So why aren't you working now?" she asked, glancing at him over her shoulder as he easily caught up to her.

"Dr. Waters told me he would take care of the calls for the afternoon."

She rolled her eyes in response. "He is such a fussy little man. Why would he do that? He often has to turn down calls."

"It makes me nervous that I'm on the job barely a week and he's already cutting back my hours."

"I think he needs to know he can trust you with his

clients," Tabitha said. "He's often bragged how he built up this practice one customer at a time. Often berated me and Jenny and Cass for not taking good enough care of them."

"I suppose," he said, though he wasn't entirely convinced that was true.

"Or he could see you as a threat." Tabitha smiled as she said the words, but Morgan wondered if that wasn't closer to the truth. But he wasn't sure what he could do about that. Some of the clients he worked with had made veiled comments about Dr. Waters and his abilities, but he had ignored it, considering it the usual gossip that happened in a community.

"Well, I'll just have to keep plugging," he said. "I'm sure he'll come around. I may be a Walsh, but I still need the job."

She shot him a quick look. "I'm guessing you overheard my comment and I'm sorry. Just feeling…bitter, I guess."

"I understand. I know some of the Walshes haven't always treated you that well."

"Given what my dad did, you can hardly blame them."

Morgan was about to tell her that wasn't what he was referring to but just then Nathan came running toward him, Brandy at his heels. His blue jeans were torn at the knees and the laces of one of his running shoes had come loose. But he was smiling for the first time in a while.

"Hey, son, your shoelace came undone," Morgan said.

Nathan looked down and stopped. Morgan walked over, knelt and tied it up for him. "There. All fixed."

Nathan frowned as he looked over at Morgan's feet

then Tabitha's. "How come you both wear cowboy boots and I have to wear sneakers?"

"You don't have to wear sneakers," Morgan said, settling back on his one leg.

"But I don't have any cowboy boots."

"Well, we'll have to buy you some," Morgan said.

"Can we go now?"

"Right now?"

Nathan nodded, his eyes bright with anticipation. "I'm done with my work and you're done with your work and Miss Tabitha is here and we can go together to town."

"I don't think Miss Tabitha will want to come," Morgan protested.

"But I want her to. She can help me pick out boots."

Tabitha lifted one shoulder in a questioning shrug. Morgan had managed to find a tiny place of peace with Nathan. A moment of happiness. It seemed like his son wanted Tabitha along.

Well, if that was what it took to keep a smile on his son's face, so be it.

"Okay. If Miss Tabitha doesn't mind…" He looked her way, surprised to see her nodding.

"I'll follow you in my truck."

"No. You ride with us," Nathan insisted.

The uncertainty on Tabitha's face mirrored his own. But taking two vehicles to town would be wasteful. "Just come with us," he said. "It'll make things easier."

For another second she hesitated, and then, seeming to see the wisdom in that, she nodded. "I'll just get my backpack and we can go." She walked into the house and returned a few moments later.

"Still no purse?" he asked as she slung the knapsack over her shoulder and walked toward his truck. He was fairly sure it was the same one she used to carry to school every day in high school.

"I like the freedom of packing whatever I need for the day on my back."

"You figuring on running away?" He hadn't meant to tease her. He blamed it on spending so much time with Tabitha. It was as if he was slipping back into his old habits.

"No. I've always liked to know that whatever I need I have with me. Survival technique from my days with my dad, I guess." She tossed the words out so casually but it reminded him of snippets of things she had told him about growing up. How often they moved. How quickly she had to be ready to leave.

She looked away and quickly got into the truck before he asked more questions or opened the door for her. Like he used to do.

Instead he opened the back door of the truck cab for his son and he clambered into his booster seat.

"I'm so excited to get some boots," he said as he tugged on the strap and buckled himself in. "I want ones like Miss Tabitha. Or maybe some red ones." He grinned, and Morgan felt a delightful warmth sift through him. Nathan seemed a lot more relaxed than he had yesterday.

Then Nathan looked at him, his smile still in place. "I'm happy Miss Tabitha is coming with us."

Morgan nodded, his good mood cooling a little.

"Me too," he said with a forced grin.

But then, as he walked around the truck and got in, he glanced over at Tabitha, who was looking down. Her hair had slid over her face, as she rifled through her backpack and pulled out her phone and studied the screen, as if avoiding looking at him.

He thought of what she'd said earlier. About her father.

"You know, I apologize for not saying anything sooner, but I was sorry to hear about your dad's passing."

Her hands stopped flicking over the screen and she looked over at him. "Thanks."

"I know it was a few years ago, but it still must be difficult at times."

"It can be. But sometimes I wish my dad looked out for me and Leanne the way your parents did for you. Especially your mother."

"What do you mean?" he asked.

"Nothing."

She turned away but Morgan sensed there was more to her comment than she let on.

But he knew he would get nothing from her now, even though the faint bitterness in her voice made him wonder what she referred to.

Chapter Six

"I like *these*." Nathan grabbed a pair of blue boots with a gray shaft and held them up to Tabitha for her inspection.

"You should ask your father," Tabitha said, pointing her chin to Morgan.

"I don't know if they have those in your size," Morgan said, hating to take the smile off his son's face.

"Can you see if they do?" Nathan handed him the boot, and for a fleeting moment Morgan caught a glimpse of yearning in his face. But it disappeared so quickly, he thought he might have imagined it.

"Is there anything I can help you with?"

Lorn Talbot's voice broke into the moment and Morgan spun around, still holding the boot Nathan had given him. The middle-aged man wore metal-rimmed glasses, his hair brushed neatly back, his shirt cinched with a narrow tie. When he smiled he showed the crooked teeth that gave him a faint lisp.

"If you could find a pair of these boots in my son's size, that would be great," Morgan said, holding out the boot.

Lorn looked momentarily taken aback. Then his polite smile reappeared. "Oh yes, I had heard that you came back with a son."

As if Morgan had picked Nathan up from the side of the road. Or at a souvenir shop.

"Let's first see what size he is." Lorn moved past Morgan and snagged a large metal plate he remembered Mr. Talbot using on him whenever he was due for new boots or shoes.

He got Nathan to stand on it, measured his foot then sat back, his arm resting on one knee. "You're in luck, boyo. I think we might have a pair left like that in your size."

Tabitha stood to one side, and as Lorn got to his feet, he glanced her way. "Ah, Miss Rennie. Did you come to pay your dad's bill?"

Lorn turned to Morgan, still grinning. "Floyd, Tabitha's father, ordered three pairs of boots before he did his own boot-scooting-boogie out of town. Guess his boots really were made for walking, except he didn't pay for them."

Morgan stifled a groan at Lorn's bad jokes. Then he saw Tabitha's features harden.

"I'm sorry my father did that to you," Tabitha said, her voice stiff, her hands clenched at her sides.

"All part of running a business, hon," Lorn said with a grin, clearly showing that there were no hard feelings. "Sometimes you're the windshield, sometimes you're the bug." Then he sauntered off to get Nathan's boots.

Tabitha gave a tight grin but it wasn't hard to see her discomfort.

Morgan wasn't sure what to say but it bothered him to see her so upset and clearly embarrassed.

"What your dad did is no reflection on you," he said,

giving in to an impulse and laying a hand on her shoulder. "You can't take all his mistakes on."

Tabitha took a breath and he felt her relax under his hand. "It's hard not to feel the humiliation of it."

"I can understand that," he said, not moving his hand. "But you have nothing to be ashamed of."

"Thanks," she said, her voice quiet as her eyes locked on his. "That means a lot."

Their gaze held for a few heartbeats longer.

Morgan tightened his grip on her shoulder, and as he lost himself in her eyes, he felt an inexpressible compulsion to kiss her.

Whoa. He was approaching dangerous territory.

Then Lorn returned and thankfully the moment was broken.

"Look at my boots." Nathan held one foot out for their inspection.

"They look great," Tabitha said, stepping away from Morgan. "How do they feel?"

Nathan strutted back and forth in the store, and when he returned, he dropped on the chair, tapping his toes together, looking proud of himself. "I'm so excited to wear these when I go riding."

"It will be a lot of fun when that happens," Tabitha said, affirming his comment.

"Thanks for your business," Lorn said as Morgan tucked his wallet back in his pocket. Then he turned to Tabitha. "And I'm sorry for what I said about your father. Was trying to make a joke and it fell kind of flat."

"Of course, Mr. Talbot. I understand," Tabitha said, giving him a kind smile.

They walked out of the store, Nathan looking down at his boots.

"That was very gracious of you," Morgan said as he held the door open for her. "It bothered me, what he said about your father."

Tabitha shrugged. "He apologized. I have to accept that."

"That's quite something to say," he said.

The flush on her cheeks surprised him. She didn't strike him as the blushing sort.

Nathan stopped in front of another store, looking at the mannequin in the window. "That lady has funny lips," he announced.

Tabitha stopped to look and chuckled with him. "Maybe she's pouting because she doesn't like the clothes she's wearing."

"Do you think that little boy likes his pants?" Nathan asked, pointing to the other mannequin standing beside the female one. "He's smiling."

"I think he does and I think they look nice."

Nathan looked down at his pants, and Morgan, once again, felt a flush of shame at the raggedness of them. But what could he do? Nathan had insisted on wearing them and not the ones he bought for him. "Mine have holes in the knees," he said.

"Well, maybe we can buy you a new pair," she said, glancing up at Morgan as if it was his fault his son looked so shabby.

"Will you help me pick them out?" Nathan looked up at Tabitha with that adoring expression he always seemed to have around her. It bothered Morgan to see the boy so attached, but he understood far too well the hold this woman could have on a guy.

"I guess I can." To her credit, Tabitha tossed a look

at him as if seeking permission. All Morgan could do was nod his acquiescence.

Nathan fist pumped, then yanked on the shop's door to go inside.

"I hope you don't mind," Tabitha said, lowering her voice as Morgan held the door open for her.

"Not at all. Maybe if you help us pick out some new clothes, he might actually wear them," he muttered.

Tabitha frowned her puzzlement as they followed Nathan into the store.

"I bought him new clothes when I picked him up from his grandmother's place," he explained. "But he won't wear them."

"Well, that makes a lot more sense," Tabitha said with a gentle smile.

"What does?"

"Why he's dressed the way he is."

"What? You thought I preferred that my son go around looking like a little homeless boy?" Morgan couldn't keep the offended tone out of his voice.

"Actually, I thought you might not notice. Which surprised me. Considering how you always dressed so nicely."

"Past tense?" he teased as they walked to the back of the store where the kids' clothing was located and Nathan stood waiting for them.

She flicked her gaze over his cowboy hat, twill shirt and worn jeans. "I like this look better." Then their eyes met and Morgan felt it again.

That faint quiver of renewed attraction. A gentle back and forth of flirtation.

"I like these pants," Nathan said, pointing to a pair of blue jeans.

To Morgan, the pants with their pre-ripped holes didn't look much different than the ones Nathan already wore. But at least these weren't as faded.

"I think they are cool, but what do you think about these?" Tabitha suggested, steering him toward another pair without rips or holes. "You probably want something different than what you already have," she said. "That way you have some choices of what to wear."

"Okay."

And that was that. Though if Morgan had his way, he would get rid of the worn and ripped blue jeans Nathan wore as soon as they got home.

"Does Dad have a budget?" Tabitha asked, shooting him a teasing glance. "Just wondering how much we can load onto the credit card."

"No budget," he said with a dismissive wave of his hand, adding a grin. "But remember, these days I seem to be only a part-time veterinarian."

Tabitha made a sympathetic face. "We'll try not to bankrupt you."

"Your generosity astounds me."

She just grinned, then turned to his son. He stood back as Nathan and Tabitha picked out two more pairs of blue jeans, a couple of pairs of cargo shorts, some T-shirts and, after some long deliberation, a cowboy hat. It was only straw but Nathan was thrilled with it.

"Thought you weren't going to bankrupt me," Morgan laughed as he pulled out his wallet again.

"Nothing a couple more hours at the vet clinic won't cover." Tabitha looked over at Nathan, who was clutching one of the crinkly bags and grinning from ear to ear as he led the way back out of the store. "I'm sure Dr.

Waters will come around sooner rather than later and you'll be able to pay off your credit card."

"Hope so. But I guess I can be thankful I can spend more time with Nathan for now."

"He seems…distant with you, if you don't mind my saying," Tabitha said.

"We're struggling."

Nathan looked so happy, however, that Morgan felt a tiny flicker of hope. Maybe, in time, they would become more connected.

"Time and miles, Ernest always says," Tabitha said as if she had read his mind. "That's the best way to connect with a horse and, I suspect, with a son you barely know."

Morgan held her gaze, recognizing the wisdom in her words. "Thanks."

She returned his look, and again, he found himself unable to look away. Unable to break the growing connection between them.

She was the first to turn her eyes away, which made him realize how she was getting under his skin. He couldn't let it happen but he wasn't sure how to stop it.

The hum of the engine was the only sound in the truck on the drive back to Morgan's place. Nathan had fallen asleep, clutching his bag of clothes, his head tipped to one side. Morgan kept his eyes on the road but occasionally she caught him looking at her as if not sure what to do about her.

Tabitha kept reliving the few moments of connection they had shared, wishing she could be stronger. Wishing Morgan didn't still have such a hold on her heart.

She had to keep her focus on what was important,

she reminded herself. Not indulge in past fantasies that she had no right to.

But in spite of her self-talk, she still stole a glance over at Morgan, disconcerted to see him watching her instead of the road.

She gave him a tight smile, determined to stay in charge.

"So, Dr. Waters. He's being difficult?" she asked, latching on to a neutral topic, pleased at the conversational tone of her voice.

He shot her a puzzled glance but seemed willing to go along.

"Yeah. I thought he would be easy to work with but he's turning into a problem."

"He's losing business, so I don't see why he's cutting your hours." Tabitha let some of her own frustration with Dr. Waters show. "I know when I first applied, Cass told me that Dr. Waters needed the help. But I guess he figured my equine specialist degree and my vet assistant program wasn't enough."

"In ranching country, with all these horses around, you'd think it would give you full-time work."

"You'd think. I sometimes wonder—" She stopped there, knowing she was veering into self-pity territory. She never knew how much was Dr. Waters just being Dr. Waters or how much was her father's reputation.

"You wonder what?"

She brushed off his question. "Would you ever consider going on your own?"

"You mean, starting my own business?" Morgan slowly shook his head. "I don't know. I'm not much of a risk taker. Don't like stepping outside of my comfort zone."

"That's what comes from growing up with money," Tabitha said, unable to resist the urge to tease him. "All your problems get swept away."

He held her gaze and she knew he was thinking of their past. "Not all of them can be fixed with money," he said.

She was silent, feeling the emotions, older and dangerous, trembling between them. Part of her so badly wanted to give in. The only time she'd ever felt like she was worth anything in her life was when she was with Morgan.

But she had to find her own way and so did he. They weren't young kids with no responsibilities anymore. Life had beaten the optimism out of both of them.

"I've had to quickly learn how to adapt," she continued. "I've been in too many situations where I'm not in charge, which made me want to find a way to change that. I don't want to be working for someone else all my life, letting them determine how many hours I work or whether I have a job at all."

"Sepp was an idiot to let you go," he said.

His defense of her gave her a small shiver of happiness. "I like to think so, though he wouldn't agree. But that's a prime example of having other people in control of my life. My father did the same thing, dragging me and my sister hither and yon, and if you're going to ask me where yon is, I can tell you. It's in the northwest corner of Saskatchewan."

"Good to know," he said, grinning. "So you want to be in control of your life. What would that life look like?"

"I want to save up enough money to build a training facility. To train horses full-time. It'll take years, though, to build up my reputation, I'm aware of that, but it's the only way I can feel like I'm in charge."

"That would require taking a risk, wouldn't it?"

"Of course it would. If there's one positive thing I learned from my father, it's that if you don't take risks, you don't get anywhere. The trick is not to take risks with other people's money." She heard the usual angry note enter her voice and she stopped herself. She had to get past all that sometime, but she knew the sooner she could pay Morgan's father his money back, the sooner that would happen.

"That's admirable. That you're willing to do that."

"You wouldn't?"

"I don't know how. Your comment about money was kind of dead-on, hard as it is to hear. My dad was harder on us but my mother spoiled us rotten. I know that now that I have a son myself. She would move mountains to make sure my twin sister, Amber, got the barrel-racing horse she wanted, no matter the cost. She pushed Dad to pay for vet school so that I could graduate without debt. I never learned to take a chance. There was always a fallback. A safety net."

His confession surprised her. As did what he said about his mother.

"But working with Dr. Waters frustrates me. He keeps pushing me away. Taking cases from me." He released a harsh laugh. "I sound like a pouting child, don't I?"

"So start something of your own," she said.

"I've thought of it."

"But it's a risk."

"Yeah. I'm not going to ask my dad for help. I would need to do it on my own."

"So do it."

He gave her an odd look. "You really are fearless, aren't you?"

"No. Just want to be in control, that's all."

He frowned, holding her gaze as if trying to delve behind her comment.

But she forced herself to look away.

Control, she reminded herself, grasping the very thing she had just said. She needed to be in control. And if she let herself weave too many daydreams around this man, she would lose that control.

Because no matter what she thought or dreamed, until her debt to his father was paid, she would feel as if that had control of her life and would determine her value and worth.

She wouldn't let that happen.

Chapter Seven

It had been a busy Saturday, Morgan thought with a feeling of satisfaction. Dr. Waters had been sick, so Morgan had taken over most of the cases at the clinic today. Now that the day was over, he was on his way to Tabitha's. She had given him instructions to her place, but Morgan knew the way. Back when they were dating, he had brought her home once. It was the only time.

Usually she would take her car, or whatever vehicle her father had bought for her to drive, and meet him wherever they were going. Though it was at the end of a long, narrow road, it was close enough to town that sometimes she walked to the highway and met him in town.

He didn't like it but she'd always been insistent.

The road made another bend and he saw a driveway ahead of him. It looked like the main road but Tabitha had been adamant that he take the second driveway. So he drove past the clearly marked one, turned another bend and saw a pair of white reflective posts marking the second driveway. It was narrower and didn't look very well maintained, but he turned down it anyway.

Then he came around a tight corner and saw the house. A grove of trees sat between it and the rest of the yard. The area around the house was tidy and neat with clipped grass and edged with brick and heavy rocks. Flower beds flanked a house that gleamed a pale yellow in the sun, trimmed with white around the windows and eaves. It looked like a fairy cottage tucked into the hillside.

He could hardly believe this was the house that Tabitha, Leanne and their father moved into when they first came here. Back then it was a dingy brown with peeling paint and a porch that looked like it was falling apart.

Now it looked sturdy and welcoming. Bright and fresh.

He got out of the truck and caught a glimpse of the barn just beyond the house. Tabitha had said she would be working in the pen, and he should go around the right side of the house to get there.

Again, she'd been very insistent.

But he ignored her orders and went around the left side. He walked past the trees, up the hill, and his heart sank. Below him lay a graveyard of cars, stacks of wood and endless boxes of unidentifiable junk. The old driveway wound through it all and he understood why Tabitha had been so adamant he take the other way in to the house.

He was dismayed at the sight. It would take weeks to clean all this up. He shook his head, wondering again at Tabitha's father and how he could have done this to his daughter.

He heard Nathan's excited voice coming from close to the barn. He knew he could get there from here but he chose to follow Tabitha's orders and walked on the opposite side of the house. He walked down a path, through the same grove of trees hiding the house from the other side of the yard, and there they were.

Nathan hung over the edge of the round pen and Tabitha stood with Stormy, flicking a tarp over her backside, holding her still with the halter rope.

To his surprise, the horse didn't even flinch.

"You've come a long ways," Morgan called out as he came near.

"It's coming."

Nathan glanced over at him, grinning, and then looked back at Tabitha.

"But I think that's all for today," Tabitha said, hanging the tarp on the fence. She led Stormy to the gate leading to the pasture, took off the halter and let her go.

Morgan was disappointed he didn't have a chance to see her in action. He would like to see what her technique was, how she worked with the horse.

Tabitha carefully climbed over the railing instead of going through the gate. The panel wobbled as she stepped over and Morgan caught her as she faltered.

For a split second she was suspended, leaning on him, her shocked glance holding his as time wheeled backward. She was seventeen and he was helping her over a fence at his parents' place after they had gone for a long walk along the pasture, up into the hills.

Just for a moment he remembered how much she had meant to him then. The dreams he had spun around her and the future he had planned for them.

Then she regained her balance and tugged her arm free, and they were both firmly back in the present again.

"Thanks," she murmured, to his surprise.

He thought she would be upset with him.

Tabitha looked over at Nathan as she slipped the halter and rope over her shoulder. "So, what do you think, buddy?"

"I think I really like Stormy," he said. "And I'm excited to ride her."

"You know it won't be for a while, though," Morgan put in.

But Nathan ignored him, looking instead at Tabitha as if the sun rose and set on her. "I'm thirsty," he said, suddenly. "Can I have a drink at your house?"

"Well… I suppose…" Tabitha hesitated, glancing at Morgan.

"Maybe Miss Tabitha wants to get to her work," Morgan advised, sensing Tabitha's uncertainty. "You've been with her all day."

"I can't wait until we get to our house," Nathan said, his gaze firmly fixed on Tabitha. "I'm thirsty now."

"That's no way to ask," Morgan reprimanded him.

"Can I *please* have a drink?" Nathan asked, correcting himself.

Tabitha looked from Morgan to Nathan, then gave in. "Sure you can."

Tabitha gave Nathan a smile and he beamed back at her. Morgan felt a surprising twinge of jealousy. His son seemed more connected to Tabitha than to him.

"I need to put this halter away and then we'll go to the house," Tabitha said.

"I'll come with you," Nathan said.

"No, that's okay—" But Nathan was already running ahead.

Morgan guessed why she had protested, but now they were all together, walking to the barn.

As they did, they skirted the bodies of a couple of old cars. The windows of the vehicles were broken and the tires flat. They weren't going anywhere soon.

"Where did those cars come from?" Nathan asked as Tabitha pulled open the door of the old hip roof barn and stepped inside.

"My dad got them from a friend," Tabitha called out from the dim interior. She came back out and closed the door, the hinges creaking out a protest.

"Do they work?"

"Nope. And they didn't when he purchased them, either."

"Then why did he buy them?"

Tabitha shoved her hands in her pockets, her steps more hurried as they walked around a couple of old farm implements and a stack of metal and wood leaning precariously against a weathered shed. "Same reason he bought all the other stuff in the yard. Thought he would use it someday for something."

Tabitha's voice held a defensive edge, and Morgan knew they weren't supposed to see this side of the place.

"Your dad bought this place when your family moved here, didn't he?"

"Yes, he did."

"I remember my father being upset because he was hoping to buy it."

"Probably one of many times that would happen, I'm sure."

He was about to ask her more but then they came near the house. "I have to say, you did an amazing job on the house and the yard."

She smiled, her shoulders lowering, her posture less defensive.

"This place has been a huge work in progress for me," Tabitha said with a faint note of pride in her voice. "Every minute I can spare, I've been fixing it up."

"You can be proud of what you've done."

"It's all about resale value," Tabitha said as she bent over to pick up a stray plastic bag that had blown into the yard and tuck it in her pocket.

"And what will you do once you sell?" He wished he could sound more casual about it, and it bothered him that he couldn't.

Tabitha paused, her eyes grazing the hills beyond the house, and for the briefest moment Morgan caught a look of yearning on her face. As if she wished things were different. But then her features straightened and she looked directly at him.

"Then I walk away from Cedar Ridge and never look back."

That hit him like a physical blow.

Did he think Tabitha would change her mind because he shared a few happy experiences?

Would he never learn?

"Are not two sparrows sold for a penny? Yet not one of them will fall to the ground outside your Father's care. And even the very hairs of your head are all numbered. So don't be afraid—you are worth more than many sparrows."

Pastor Blakely looked up as he closed the Bible, a gentle smile on his face as he looked out over the congregation. "I always get such comfort from this piece of Scripture," he said. "Sparrows have never held much value, and yet God is telling us that He watches over them too. And that if He watches over them, how much more does He watch over us? How valuable does that make each of us?"

Tabitha clung to her open Bible, the pastor's words resonating with her.

She looked down at the Bible in her lap, shaking her head at the sight of the scrambled letters in front of her. Most of her life had been spent making connections between the squiggles she saw on the paper and the words they represented. Her memory and recall were amazing but they had all been coping skills she'd perfected in her lifelong struggle with dyslexia. Something that was only diagnosed when she was in junior high, a couple of years before she had come to Cedar Ridge.

A caring teacher had finally explained to her why reading was so difficult for her compared to her classmates. Tabitha had found out that there were various levels and kinds of dyslexia, and while hers wasn't as extreme as some, it was still a tremendous amount of work for her to read. Her dyslexia was exacerbated by the constant moving. So when Tabitha, her sister, Leanne, and their father had moved to Cedar Ridge, it was simply one more barrier, one more mountain to climb. She'd struggled along as much as she could, hiding her difficulties from everyone, including Morgan. For the most part she managed, and she and Morgan had never shared any classes.

Then she got Morgan's mother as an English teacher in the first term of Grade Twelve and things went downhill from there. Mrs. Walsh never approved of Tabitha as Morgan's girlfriend, and Tabitha resorted to her usual antics in class to hide her disability and her frustration with Mrs. Walsh's assessment of her. A month later, in utter frustration, she'd quit school. Six months later Mrs. Walsh had confronted her.

"We are valuable. Precious. Loved," the pastor preached, underlining what the passage said.

Tabitha heard the words and, once again, fought to make them her own. To weave them into her life. Even in church, around people who were followers of God, she battled feelings of inferiority.

When Morgan came to pick Nathan up at her house yesterday, she had tried, in vain, to keep the mess of the rest of the yard away from him. She could still feel the shame as she saw the mess through Morgan's eyes.

Yes, she felt like saying, *this is what my life with my father was like. Looks good on the one hand, but there is a darker, messier side.*

And that's why I need to leave here, she thought. *I don't need to be reminded every time I turn around of who I am and where I come from.*

Despite those thoughts, her eyes sought out Morgan and Nathan sitting with Morgan's father. They sat one pew ahead and across the aisle, and she could watch them without them knowing. Nathan was looking down, probably staring at his new cowboy boots, rocking slightly. Morgan's attention seemed to be split between the pastor and his son, and every time he looked at Nathan, Tabitha saw the sorrow on his face.

Tabitha wanted to assure him that it would take time for Nathan to get to know and trust him.

The sight of Morgan wanting to connect with his boy also brought back memories of when they were dating. He could be so kind and protective.

She swallowed down an unexpected and unwelcome ache at what she had lost and forced her attention back to the pastor. Morgan was part of her past and he was settling here in Cedar Ridge.

Her future meant putting Cedar Ridge and all it represented behind her.

The rest of the service flowed along, but as the congregation stood for the last song, Tabitha felt her heart drop.

It was her favorite song. One that Morgan used to hum when he was in a good mood.

"You are worth, more than all gold, My dearest treasure of wealth untold. I see you child, as I want you to be, Perfect and lovely, whole and free."

To her shame Tabitha felt her throat thicken at the familiar words.

My dearest treasure of wealth untold.

She held on to the words as the old weariness washed over her. She was so tired of the stress of living with her father's shadow, and her own lack of abilities. She was tired of always feeling unworthy.

And now, with Morgan around, she was reminded of a life that had been within her grasp. A good life with a man who had roots and family.

Perfect and lovely, whole and free.

She drew in a trembling breath, and as the last notes of the song resonated through the building, she tried to find a quick escape. She didn't want to run into Morgan while she felt so emotionally shaky.

Trouble was, she wasn't sitting in her usual spot because she had waited for Leanne, who had told her at the last minute that she couldn't come. So she had to sit farther ahead. Now she was caught between two elderly women who weren't in any rush to finish their conversation with the people in the pew in front of them.

Which put her in the awkward position of ending up right beside Morgan and Nathan when she finally managed to step into the aisle.

"Miss Tabitha," Nathan cried out, grabbing her hand. "I'm wearing my new boots. See?" He held out his foot for her inspection. "And my new pants and shirt."

"You look very spiffy," she said, still gathering her composure.

"We're going to my uncle Cord's house for lunch. Grandpa is coming. You should come too."

Tabitha was at a momentary loss for words. There was no way she could face Boyce Walsh across a dinner table when she had spent so much time trying to stay off his radar.

"Maybe Miss Tabitha has other plans, Nathan," Morgan jumped in, giving Tabitha an out.

She didn't know whether to feel hurt or relieved, which in turn exasperated her. She didn't like how being around Morgan confused her so much.

"I want you to come," Nathan said, his voice rising and falling in a classic put-out child's whine as he grabbed Tabitha's hand. "Please. You can tell Grandpa Boyce about my horse."

"Yes, I'd love to hear about this horse."

And there was Boyce Walsh. His eyes holding nothing but a sparkle, a grin lighting up his face.

"I think you should join us, Tabitha," Boyce continued. "You can tell us how the training is going with Stormy. I know Cord and Ella won't mind."

"What won't we mind?" Ella joined them, her soft brown eyes flicking from Nathan, still holding Tabitha's hand, to Boyce.

"We just invited Tabitha for lunch."

"I think that's a great idea," Ella said, smiling at Tabitha, her expression welcoming. "We can serve you for a change instead of you waiting on us."

Tabitha knew Ella meant it as a gentle joke but somehow it underlined the differences between them. Ella, a renowned artist who had reinvented herself and was gaining praise for her new work. And Tabitha. Ex-waitress and daughter of the local loser.

"Please come," Nathan said, still holding her hand. "You can meet my new cousins. Paul, Suzy and Oliver. Suzy teases me but Paul says she teases everyone."

Tabitha was even more torn. She knew Nathan was growing attached to her, but to refuse his, Boyce's and Ella's invitations seemed rude.

"You know how to get to the ranch," Morgan said, taking the decision out of her hands. "We'll see you there." He held his hand out to Nathan. "Why don't we go ahead and get lunch ready for Miss Tabitha?"

But Nathan simply walked away, spurning Morgan's gesture.

Tabitha saw the hurt on Morgan's face and she laid a gentle hand on his shoulder. It was only supposed to be a show of comfort. But when he looked at her and their eyes met, a quiver of attraction grew deep in her soul.

She didn't want to break the connection. In fact, she wanted to put her other hand on his other shoulder, like she used to. Tease him. Like she used to.

Her breath caught and it wasn't until they were jostled by someone wanting to get past them that the moment was broken.

He looked momentarily taken aback and then, to her dismay, he stepped back, his expression hardening. Then he strode away.

Tabitha struggled with her roiling emotions. What was she doing? Whatever it was, it definitely wasn't fair to Morgan.

She'd had her chance with him and she'd made her choice.

What if I told him what actually happened and why?

She held that thought as she made her way through the crowd of people on the way to the door, taking her time.

Then she stepped outside, heading toward her truck, which was parked right beside the church. That was when she saw him.

Morgan stood by his mother's grave. His hand rested on the stone, his head down. He swiped at his cheeks, as if he was crying, and the sight cut into her soul. He missed his mother.

Then someone stopped her to ask a question about her cat. Tabitha obliged, thankful for the chance to pull herself back to ordinary.

By the time she was done, Morgan and Nathan were gone.

And Tabitha knew there was no way she would be able to tell him what had really happened.

Not ever.

Chapter Eight

Tabitha slowed her truck down as she approached the driveway leading to the Walsh ranch house. She still had a chance to change her mind and go back home.

But the thought of letting Nathan down kept her going. He had asked her to come. She knew better than to disappoint a young child.

She turned into the driveway. She had been to the Walsh house a couple of times before, so she knew what to expect. The driveway split after passing the small house to her right that she guessed Ella lived in until she and Cord were married.

Tabitha drove on past a copse of trees, turned a corner and there it was. The Walsh home.

Except it looked different. The lower half of the house was now covered in rough stone, which also framed the doorway. The house had wooden siding instead of dusky blue vinyl siding and it looked like the windows had changed.

The wraparound veranda was also different. Tabitha suspected Cord's now-deceased wife, Lisa, had been responsible for the updates.

But while the house had been redone, the amazing view was as timeless as she remembered.

The ranch house sat on a rise that overlooked a valley. Beyond the valley rose the Rocky Mountains, majestic and imposing. Tabitha knew the house overlooked only a portion of the Walsh ranch. But it was an impressive portion.

She parked her truck beside Morgan's and the other two vehicles. She suspected one belonged to Boyce, the other to Cord.

She wondered what Cord thought of her coming for dinner. While she and Morgan were dating, his brother had kept his distance. Tabitha knew Cord wasn't crazy about her. In fact, shortly after she broke up with Morgan, she had seen Cord in town. He hadn't said anything, but the look of fury on his face toward her was enough. Tabitha left town shortly after that so she didn't have to face him again.

Since she came back, she'd seen Cord in town now and again, and he was always unfailingly polite, but she'd never been able to erase that look from her memory.

Maybe she should go.

She reached for her keys still dangling in the ignition when the door burst open and three children came running out. A large dog she hadn't seen before came bounding down from the veranda to join them.

She saw Nathan waving at her, his face full of joy as he ran to her truck.

Paul and Suzy came down the stairs too, but they held back, as if unsure what to do with the woman who usually served them French fries and ice cream and now stood in their yard.

"You came," Nathan said as she closed the door of her truck and slipped her bag over her shoulder. "My... my... Morgan said you might not and not to be disappointed."

That was the second time she'd heard him make that slip. Saying "my" and then switching to "Morgan," as if he was about to say "my dad" but didn't dare.

Tabitha looked at Paul and Suzy and waved at them. "Hey, you two."

"I wish you could paint my face like a cat again," Suzy said, bouncing up to her, her pigtails bouncing. "Like you did at the fair."

"I don't have the paints with me, otherwise I could." Tabitha had manned the booth for the Brand and Grill at the spring fair in the park.

Then Suzy grabbed her hand and pulled. "We were waiting for you and I'm hungry."

"I see that," Tabitha said, allowing the girl to drag her onto the veranda.

"What took you so long?" Suzy demanded as Paul opened the door for both of them.

"Temperamental truck" was all she said. She hadn't been able to start her truck after church and had needed a boost. Tony Schlegal had been more helpful boosting her car than he'd been at the hardware store. Hopefully it would start again when it was time to leave.

She heard voices and laughter when she came into the house. As she tugged her sandals off, she glanced around the hallway. It too had been renovated. The floor was done in tile with an inlaid compass. The colors were now fresh aqua and white.

"Miss Tabitha is finally here," Suzy called out as

she flounced into the kitchen, Paul and Nathan trailing behind her.

Ella stood at the quartz kitchen counter mixing something up in a bowl. Her hair was pulled back in a loose ponytail and she wore a gauzy white blouse with intricate pleats at the yoke and top of the sleeves. Very artsy, Tabitha thought.

She looked up when Tabitha arrived. "Hey. Glad you came," she said, her voice friendly and welcoming.

"Thanks for the invite. Can I help you with anything?"

"I'm just putting the finishing touches on this potato salad and then we can eat." She nodded toward the large table beside the kitchen where Morgan, Cord and Boyce sat. "Why don't you join the men?"

"And talk about cows and tractors and rodeo?"

Ella chuckled at that. "I think it's mostly rodeo talk these days. Something about getting the arena looked at by their cousin Reuben. They want to see if it's worth finishing."

Ah, the unfinished arena. The dark cloud over Tabitha's life.

"I'll stay here until you're done," Tabitha said, leaning her elbows on the kitchen island.

The kids were playing a game in the family room located just off the dining area. Toys were scattered over the floor and music played softly in the background. Quite a change from when Mrs. Walsh lived here, Tabitha thought.

Pictures and wooden plaques with inspirational sayings hung on previously stark and bare walls. A rough bouquet of wildflowers, shoved in an antique watering can on the counter, was parked beside a bright striped bowl of fruit and a matching tray that held odds and ends.

Mrs. Walsh kept everything achingly neat and tidy. The house was always immaculate and beautifully decorated.

But this house looked like a home.

"The kids were excited to see you again," Ella said, setting the bowl aside and washing her hands. "Suzy was hoping you would bring the face paints along."

"As if I could compete with you," Tabitha returned. "How is the art coming? I heard you were getting ready for a new show."

"You heard correctly."

Tabitha could hear the question in Ella's voice and smiled. "I used to work at the Brand and Grill. Where there are no secrets."

Ella chuckled. "And I imagine you heard most of them."

"I try to be discreet. Though I have thought of starting a gossip column for the local paper."

"I'd read it," Ella said, drying her hands on a towel. "Be a great way to find out more about my new home and community."

"You like it here?" she asked, curious as to Ella's reaction.

"I do. The people are welcoming, the town is just the right size and it's a great place to raise kids." Ella grinned. "You know, the usual sales pitches real-estate agents use to sell homes in places people are reluctant to move to. Make it about the kids." Then Ella shot her a curious glance. "I understand you're not originally from around here either?"

"Nope. No grandparents buried in the cemetery."

Ella looked puzzled as she picked up the bowl of potato salad.

"That's the usual cliché when talking about whether you were born and raised here or are from somewhere else," Tabitha explained.

"So when did you move here?" Ella walked over to the table where the men were sitting and set the bowl beside plates that held buns, cold cuts and another that held cookies and bars.

"I was in junior high when we came to town."

"Whoa, that must have been rough."

Tabitha shot a glance at Morgan, who had been talking to his brother but now looked up.

"It was hard on her," Morgan added, getting up to pull a chair out for Tabitha. "No thanks to me and Amber."

"What do you mean?" Ella asked her future brother-in-law.

"Let's say we didn't make it the easiest on her."

"That's because you had the biggest crush on her," Boyce put in. Then he gave Tabitha a gentle smile. "Sorry, but it was true."

Tabitha could hardly speak. She was so surprised to hear Boyce speak so openly about his son's relationship with her.

"He was definitely smitten," Cord chimed in, giving Tabitha a careful look.

She wasn't sure how to interpret all of this.

"I wish Amber was easier on you, is all," Boyce continued. "I always felt like I should apologize for her behavior."

"Amber had her own stuff," Morgan put in.

"Well, if your mother hadn't spoiled the two of you rotten, she might not have had *stuff*," Boyce grumbled.

"Oversharing, guys," Cord said, shooting a warning

glance around the table. "I don't think Tabitha needs to hear all the Walsh family dysfunctions."

Tabitha was amazed at the completely unexpected comments. Boyce apologizing for his daughter? Mentioning dysfunction in the Walsh family?

"I think we can eat now," Ella called out. "Kids! Time to come to the table."

They scrambled to their feet and hurried over.

"Is Oliver napping?" Morgan asked, looking around as Suzy and Paul found their places.

"Yeah, he's always so tired after church." Cord pulled a chair out for Ella and settled Suzy in another one. "And grumpy."

"Like his dad," Ella teased. Cord tugged her ponytail in reply and sat down.

"I want to sit by Miss Tabitha," Nathan announced as he dragged a chair away from the table. "You sit here," he said, pointing to an empty chair beside him.

Which would put her right beside Morgan.

"Don't you want to sit between your dad and me?" she suggested.

Nathan glanced over at Morgan, looking as if he was considering the idea. Then he shook his head. "No. I want to sit with you."

Again embarrassment washed over Tabitha, but as she sat beside Morgan, another feeling superseded that emotion.

Here she was again. Sitting beside Morgan at the table in the Walsh house with members of his family.

She remembered all too well how much she enjoyed being here once Morgan dared tell his family they were dating. For a few months, before she dropped out of school and before things fell apart, she felt a part of a family that had roots and belonged to a community.

Things she had always longed to be a part of.

But thanks to his mother, her father and her own past with Morgan, it was not to be.

"Let's pray," Boyce said, looking around the table, his gaze resting for a few seconds on Tabitha.

Then everyone reached out their hands. She took Nathan's and then, after a moment's hesitation, Morgan's. His hand was warm. Rougher than it used to be. The hands of a man, not a young boy.

And as his fingers curled around hers, she couldn't stop from seeking out his face.

Only to find him looking at her as his features softened.

And when his hand tightened around hers, Tabitha thought her heart would burst.

Morgan sat back in the wooden chair on the deck, a feeling of satisfaction washing over him as he looked out over the view. Good lunch. Good company.

Tabitha sat upright in her chair beside him, her hands clasped tightly on her lap. She looked tense. Did being around his family do that to her?

Or did his presence cause it?

Cord had settled on a rattan sofa beside Tabitha's chair. Boyce had gone back to his house in town, claiming that he needed a nap. The kids were playing on the swings and play center that Cord had set up a month or so ago. Nathan seemed happy enough to join them. Another small victory.

Though he'd been back to the family home since he

left, it still shook him to see the changes that Lisa had made when she and Cord got married.

"If you have the time, Morgan, I'd like you to check out a cow that's having some trouble," Cord said, clasping his hands behind his head, his one foot resting on his knee.

"Surely you're not going to make the poor guy work on his day off," Ella teased as she sat down beside Cord, cuddling up against him.

"He doesn't work that hard," Cord returned, giving Ella a gentle smile as he fingered a strand of hair away from her face. "He can help his big brother out."

Morgan felt a flicker of jealousy at the sight. He knew his brother had traveled his own dark road to get to this place. Losing his wife in childbirth, trying to raise three kids on his own.

Ella coming into his life was an answer to many prayers sent up by his father.

"I don't mind," Morgan said, leaning back. He looked over to where Nathan was playing with Suzy and Paul. The sound of his laughter floated back to him and it made him smile to see his son happy for a change.

"And how is the horse training with Stormy coming along, Tabitha?" Cord asked.

"She's headstrong but we're working on that." Tabitha's voice sounded strained.

"Do you seriously think you'll get her to the point that Nathan can ride her?"

The incredulity in his brother's voice annoyed Morgan.

"Tabitha knows what she's doing," he snapped.

Cord shot him a surprised look. "I'm sure she does. Ernest taught her, after all."

Tabitha spoke up. "A horse like Stormy might not be the best mount for a child now, but in time—"

"She sure looked explosive to me when Ernest brought her over," Cord said, shaking his head. "I think it'll take way too much work to turn her into a kid's horse. Waste of time, if you ask me."

"We didn't ask you." Morgan shot a warning look at his brother.

"We'll have to see how it goes," Tabitha said, her voice tight.

Morgan wanted to reassure her that he thought she was capable.

But before he could say or do anything, she stood. "I should go," she said, turning to Ella and Cord. "Thanks for a wonderful lunch. I enjoyed it."

"You don't have to leave yet, do you?" Ella protested.

"I should. Thanks again for lunch. It was delicious." She gave Ella and Cord a tight smile, then walked past them all around the corner.

Morgan waited until she was gone then turned on his brother.

"You could have said that more tactfully." Morgan blew out a sigh, shaking his head at his brother's disappointing insensitivity. "I'll be back."

Cord held his angry gaze, his own expression impassive. But Morgan saw the warning in his eyes and knew that his brother still had his concerns about Tabitha.

Tabitha was still in her truck, grimacing as she turned the key. The engine turned over once. Then again.

"Won't it start?" he asked as he came to stand by the truck's open window.

She wouldn't look at him as she shook her head. "Nope. Might need a boost."

Morgan tapped his hand on the door of his truck, trying to find the right words. "I'm sorry about Cord. I don't know what's gotten into him."

"I think I do."

"What do you mean?"

"Nothing. It's just…nothing." She opened the door of her truck and he stepped back. "I have a set of booster cables if you don't mind helping me out."

He wanted to ask her more but he sensed she wasn't going to tell him.

So he opened the hood, then went to move his truck closer. She was ready with the booster cables when he turned his truck off and got out.

"You put the red cable on the positive?" she asked.

"Make sure you keep the clamps far away from each other" was all he said as he got ready to hook up the negative post.

She nodded, keeping the black cord well away from the red. She had that snappy look on her face that he remembered all too well. It was her habitual expression the first year she was in school.

He sighed as she got in and started her truck. It turned over once, twice, and then the engine roared to life.

He made quick work of unhooking the cables before she got out, rolled them up and handed them to her. She avoided his gaze, which annoyed him and frustrated him simultaneously. He thought they had been getting somewhere. When she agreed to come here after church, he'd taken that as a positive sign.

But now she was reserved, withdrawn and angry.

"Maybe let it keep running for a while when you get home," Morgan said. "Make sure the battery is charged up good and proper."

"I will. Thanks." Again, minimal eye contact. "Say goodbye to Nathan for me, please."

She put her truck in gear and he stepped away. She drove off leaving Morgan behind, annoyed and confused. He thought about how Cord had treated her. What his father had said about Amber and him.

Both were a good reminder to him why Tabitha was leaving. He didn't blame her.

And he knew it was for the best. She was starting to get to him and he couldn't let that happen again.

Chapter Nine

Tabitha kept pulling Stormy's halter, keeping her pressure steady.

"What do you want her to do now?" Nathan asked from behind the fence.

"I want her to move her back feet and I won't let go until she does." Tabitha fought down a beat of frustration at the horse's stubbornness, remembering Ernest's constant mantra. *To hurry is to lose control.*

She and Nathan had spent the morning going over his schoolwork. It was exhausting for her, but she wouldn't admit it.

When he was done, they drove to her place to work with Stormy some more. She'd texted Morgan to let him know where she was. To her surprise, he had shown up a few minutes later, saying that Dr. Waters had said he could handle the rest of the calls himself.

Again.

Tabitha could tell Morgan was frustrated but he also seemed happy to be with Nathan. He had joined them at the corrals. While part of Tabitha was pleased he was there, she also felt very self-conscious suddenly. Ever since Sunday, Cord's questions about Stormy taunted her and made her second-guess what she was doing.

Was she truly wasting everyone's time by working with this horse, as Cord had inferred?

The question haunted her and was all the worse because it only underlined her own concerns.

"She's persistent, isn't she?" Morgan asked.

"I just need to be *more* persistent." Tabitha struggled to keep the snappy tone out of her voice. Yesterday when she came back home, second thoughts and doubts dogged her again, and she wondered if Morgan had the same misgivings about her abilities as his brother.

Then, finally, Stormy moved her back feet away from Tabitha and she immediately released the rope, petting the horse, stroking her side and encouraging her. Then she did the same thing all over again to reinforce the lesson. This time it took only a few minutes.

"She's catching on," Morgan said.

"Morgan found me a saddle, Miss Tabitha," Nathan piped up. "And it fits me."

Tabitha glanced over at Morgan, looking puzzled.

"I found one at the ranch. Used to be Amber's. Cord is fixing it up for Nathan. One of the stirrups needs repairs and it needs to be oiled."

"That's great," Tabitha said, wondering if Morgan wasn't pushing things too quickly.

"I'm excited to use it," Nathan said, adding one more burden to Tabitha. "When can I?"

She could hear his frustration. She knew exactly how badly he wanted to ride his mother's horse.

It won't happen.

She pushed the unhelpful voice aside and concentrated on what she was doing, wishing, as she often did, that she didn't have an audience.

After half an hour of watching little happen, Nathan jumped down off the fence. "I want to go for a walk around the yard," he said. "Can I?"

"Not by yourself, sweetie. Your dad will have to go with you."

"Okay." Nathan turned to Morgan. "Can you come?"

"If it's okay with Tabitha, sure."

It wasn't really, but Morgan had already seen the mess on the yard. It wouldn't be a surprise.

"Just be careful. There's a lot of…stuff." While she wasn't keen on having Morgan and Nathan see the mess that was her yard close-up, she was grateful for the reprieve.

Sunday had created such a maelstrom of emotions in her, she was thankful she didn't have to work in the vet clinic with Morgan this morning. That gave her a chance to breathe.

It had been so difficult to sit beside Morgan at the house that she'd once visited when they'd dated. To hold his hand while his father prayed over the meal. To hear Boyce bring up her and Morgan's old relationship.

And having him standing by the fence, patiently watching her as she second-guessed everything she was doing, only made it harder to concentrate.

They soon left and it was just her and the horse.

Half an hour later, Morgan and Nathan were still gone. And Tabitha was reasonably satisfied with the progress she'd made with Stormy. The horse had a long way to go, but things were moving in the right direction.

She let Stormy go into the pasture, then clambered

over the fence to see where Morgan and Nathan had got to.

A few minutes later she found them by an old car. Nathan was inside the car, pretending to drive it. Morgan was grinning at the sight.

"This is an awesome vehicle," Nathan called out. "Does it still work?"

"No, it doesn't," Tabitha said with a smile at the boy's pleasure.

"I'm thirsty," Nathan announced.

"I've got some lemonade and cookies in the house," Tabitha answered.

Nathan spun the steering wheel of the car one more time, then got out, following Tabitha and Morgan through a maze of boxes and stuff. Once again Tabitha had to resist the urge to explain all the junk. Resist the embarrassment that rose up at the unsightly mess.

"You have a lot of things," Nathan said, pausing to check out an old bathtub full of boxes of belts and rusted-out machinery parts. "It's like a treasure hunt."

"If rust and metal is your treasure," Tabitha said. "I hope to get it cleaned up soon, before I sell the place."

She felt she had to explain. Just in case Morgan thought she didn't see it for herself.

"That will be a lot of work for you," Morgan said.

"I prefer not to worry about it," Tabitha said, glancing around the old truck bodies, pieces of tractors and boxes of junk they passed on their way to her house. "I'll deal with it once I'm finished in the house."

Tabitha followed Nathan into the kitchen, cringing at the sight of the counterless kitchen, the patchy spackling job she'd done on the backsplash.

She pulled open the refrigerator and took out the

lemonade she had made for Nathan and put it on the table. She snagged a couple of glasses from the cupboard and poured the lemonade in. Nathan slurped his down right away.

"Can I go outside?" he asked.

"What do you say to Tabitha first?" Morgan reprimanded.

Nathan frowned at him, but turned to Tabitha. "Thanks. Now can I go?"

"Sure, but be careful," Tabitha said. She turned to Morgan.

"Some lemonade?" she asked, holding up a cup.

"No, thanks," he said, looking around the house. "I like what you did here."

She smiled at his approval. "Thanks. I hope the future buyer sees the potential."

"Right. Well, as for Stormy, what do you think we should do?"

The businesslike tone had returned to Morgan's voice and she suspected it had much to do with her talk of selling the house. She let the thought linger. Could she keep the house? There was no debt or mortgage against it. Her father had life insurance against the loan, which was paid out when he died.

But then she looked over at Morgan and the set of his jaw. She quashed that thought. There was too much between them, and besides, he had Nathan to think of now.

"I think you're going to have to tell him that it will be a while before he can ride Stormy."

"I'm inclined to agree with you." Morgan sighed.

Tabitha heard the sorrow in his voice. She knew how badly Morgan wanted to be able to do this for a son who was so distant from him.

FREE Merchandise is 'in the Cards' for you!

Dear Reader,

We're giving away FREE MERCHANDISE!

Seriously, we'd like to reward you for reading this novel by giving you **FREE MERCHANDISE** worth over $20 retail. And no purchase is necessary!

You see the Jack of Hearts sticker above? Paste that sticker in the box on the Free Merchandise Voucher inside. Return the Voucher today... and we'll send you Free Merchandise!

Thanks again for reading one of our novels—and enjoy your Free Merchandise with our compliments!

Pam Powers

Pam Powers

P.S. Look inside to see what Free Merchandise is **"in the cards"** for you!

W

e'd like to send you two free books like the one you are enjoying now. Your two books have a combined cover price of over $10 retail, but they are yours to keep absolutely FREE! We'll even send you 2 wonderful surprise gifts. You can't lose!

REMEMBER: Your Free Merchandise, consisting of **2 Free Books** and **2 Free Gifts**, is worth over $20 retail! No purchase is necessary, so please send for your Free Merchandise today.

Get TWO FREE GIFTS!

We'll also send you 2 wonderful FREE GIFTS (worth about $10 retail), in addition to your 2 Free books!

Visit us at:
www.ReaderService.com

YOUR FREE MERCHANDISE INCLUDES…

2 FREE Books **AND** 2 FREE Mystery Gifts

FREE MERCHANDISE VOUCHER

2 FREE
BOOKS
and
2 FREE
GIFTS

Please send my Free Merchandise, consisting of
2 Free Books and **2 Free Mystery Gifts**.
I understand that I am under no obligation to buy
anything, as explained on the back of this card.

❏ I prefer the regular-print edition
105/305 IDL GLTL

❏ I prefer the larger-print edition
122/322 IDL GLTL

Please Print

FIRST NAME

LAST NAME

ADDRESS

APT.#   CITY

STATE/PROV.   ZIP/POSTAL CODE

NO PURCHASE NECESSARY!

LI-517-FMIVY17

"How about if you take him out riding on a horse you can trust? Get him on another horse and maybe that will be enough of a distraction that he's not thinking about riding Stormy so much."

Morgan nodded slowly as if considering the idea.

"It would be an outing with your son," Tabitha pressed. "A chance to connect on another level."

"I could use the connection."

"I think he's softening to you," Tabitha said. "I don't know if you've noticed, but there were a couple of times where he almost referred to you as 'my dad' but caught himself."

"Well, that's something," Morgan said, giving her a wry smile.

"It's like training a horse. You need to be patient but persistent."

Morgan's smile shifted as he held her eyes. "This matters to you, doesn't it?"

"Yes. Of course. I don't like seeing kids disconnected from their fathers."

"Were you? Disconnected from your father, I mean."

She slid her eyes away from his probing glance. "I loved my dad. He was a lot of fun. But fathers like him are more interesting when they're someone else's. My love for him was worn away one scheme, one lie, one disappointment at a time."

Suddenly, to her surprise and dismay, she felt Morgan's hand on her face. His fingers curled around her cheek as he gently turned her to him.

"You're not your father, you know."

She could only stare at him, a chill slipping down her spine. How did he know that was how she felt?

"You are your own person," he continued. "And while

I'm sure you loved him in your own way, you don't have to take on who he was. You don't have to make up for who he was."

"I don't know if you realize who he was and what he did," Tabitha said, unable to keep the bitter tone out of her voice. "I get reminded enough." She wanted to look away and pull away from his touch, but it felt so good to have his hand holding her. It had been so long since she felt that anyone saw her for herself.

Morgan's fingers caressed her cheek as his eyes traveled over her features. "Is that why you want to leave?"

She held his curious gaze, then gave in to an impulse and lifted her hand, covering his, giving herself a few more seconds of this connection.

"I have to leave" was all she could say. "It's the only way I can live with myself."

"Why?"

She wondered if he would truly understand her reasons.

"Please, tell me."

She thought back to his father. So caring. So considerate.

The difference was too great. So she shook her head and turned away, breaking the moment between them.

"My dad wants to go riding with me tomorrow." Nathan was sitting in Tabitha's truck, looking out the window as they drove down the road to the Walsh ranch Wednesday afternoon. Tabitha had worked at the clinic that morning, then had picked up Nathan from Cord's place. Ella had been watching the kids. Thankfully Cord wasn't there. She didn't want to face his condemnation again.

She and Nathan had spent the afternoon with Stormy and it had gone well.

"I don't think I want to go riding."

"Why not? I think it's a great idea," Tabitha said. "You like riding, and Stormy won't be ready to ride for a while, so you may as well ride another horse."

Nathan was quiet, looking down at his boots. "What if he changes his mind? What if he doesn't take me?"

Tabitha thought of something Nathan had said to her last week about his mother telling him that Morgan didn't keep his promises. At that time she had told herself not to get involved and she still knew that to be true, but it bothered her that Morgan was trying so hard and Nathan couldn't see it.

"Your dad cares about you a lot," she said, looking ahead at the road, struggling to find the right thing to say that could help these two. "He is taking good care of you. He really loves you."

"My mom said he didn't."

"What?" Tabitha shot him a quick glance, surprised to see the little boy's deep scowl.

"My mom said he didn't love me. That's why he didn't come and visit me. Or live with my mom and me and be a family. He didn't want to have me."

The words tumbled out of Nathan's mouth in a rush. It was as if he'd heard them so many times, he could spout them off by heart.

Shock and anger surged through Tabitha. How could a mother say that to her child?

"Your father does love you," Tabitha said, wanting to reassure him. "He wanted so badly to visit you but—" She caught herself there, knowing that her anger with Nathan's mother would cloud her words and her judgment. No matter her opinion, Gillian was still his mother.

"He didn't try," Nathan snapped. "If he did try, why didn't I ever see him? I wanted to, but my mommy said my daddy didn't care." Then, to her dismay, his lower lip trembled and Tabitha caught the glint of tears in his eyes.

The poor kid.

Tabitha pulled over to the side of the road, stopped the truck, unbuckled her seat belt and scooched over. She put her arm around his thin shoulders. Nathan melted against her and started to cry.

Tabitha's heart shifted with pain and she pulled the sobbing boy close.

"He *did* try to see you," Tabitha said, stroking his hair, holding him tight, bewildered at the maternal feelings he raised in her. Surprised how her heart broke at the sound of his tears, at the shake of his shoulders under her arms.

Please, Lord, give me the right words, she prayed. *Help me to help this poor child. And his father.*

"He did try," she repeated. "But your mother was so busy traveling all over the place, going to rodeos. He couldn't always find you."

Nathan sniffed as his sobs slowly eased off.

"He wanted to find you," she insisted. "But it's hard when someone is moving around so much."

He lifted his head, his glance latching on hers as if testing her to see if she was telling the truth. "Is that for real?"

"It is. I know it. Morgan—your dad," she corrected herself, "is a good man and he wants to be a really good father."

Nathan seemed to consider this, and Tabitha pressed the point.

"He wanted to be with you," she continued. "He loves you so much. But every time he thought you were in one place, you moved." She was winging it with what she was saying, but she also knew that Morgan would have moved heaven and earth to find his son. "And when he finally found you, he brought you here. To his home. Where he grew up because he wanted you to have a real home."

"A home here in Cedar Ridge?"

"Yes."

"And he won't move?"

"No. He has family here. A dad, a brother who has kids, and uncles and aunts. He belongs here." As she listed off Morgan's connections to Cedar Ridge, Tabitha couldn't stop the usual glimmer of envy. Morgan was so rooted here. Unlike Nathan's mother, who had always been on the move. Seeming to be avoiding something she preferred not to face.

And what about me? Aren't I doing the same thing?

The words floated through her subconscious.

Aren't I trying to outrun what I should face?

Her heart shifted its rhythm as the words accused her.

No. She wasn't. She had to clean up her father's mess. Give herself a reason to hold her head up, redeem herself and leave.

She needed to finish the house, clean up the yard and sell, then start fresh somewhere else.

The list of reasons seemed to calm and center her.

"So my dad is going to stay here?" Nathan sniffed, swiping the back of his hand over his nose.

Tabitha reached into her backpack and pulled out a package of tissues. "Your dad is staying here," she said, handing him a couple. "I know that for a fact. This is where he grew up and always wanted to live."

Nathan wiped his nose and drew in a shaky breath. "And he loves me?"

"He loves you a lot. Your father is a good man and a good father."

And listen to me. If he's such a good man, why am I leaving? I know things are growing between us.

She shook her head as if to eradicate the memories, put her seat belt back on and put the truck in gear.

Stay focused on the next job, she reminded herself. *Just do what comes next. Don't think too far ahead. Don't plan too far ahead.*

It was how she got through all the disappointments in her life. The false hopes. Staying in control and sticking with her plan.

Morgan and Nathan were only a momentary distraction.

But as she drove away, she couldn't get rid of the idea that they were more than that. Much more.

Chapter Ten

"Not the best weather for riding," Cord said as he helped Morgan saddle up the last horse.

Morgan squinted up at the low-hanging clouds scudding across the sky. "As long as it's not raining, we should be okay."

"I think it's a great idea that you and Nathan go out riding together," Cord said, yanking on the cinch strap to tighten it. "It's a good way to spend some time with him. I'm not so sure it's a good idea to take Tabitha along."

Morgan glanced over his shoulder.

Tabitha had Nathan astride Bronco, a bay gelding, and was leading him around the corral, giving him a chance to get used to the horse. Cord had insisted that she was bombproof and Morgan believed him, but he was still thankful for Tabitha's help.

"Nathan wouldn't come unless she came along too."

Morgan read disapproval in his brother's shrug. He understood Cord's concerns, and while he felt stuck between pleasing his son and guarding his heart, pleasing his son was winning out.

Trouble was, the wall around his heart was slowly wearing away the more time he and Tabitha spent together.

"Look, I know you don't like her—"

"I like her fine. She's a great girl." Cord leaned one arm against the horse, looking past him to where Tabitha was leading Nathan around on the horse. "She's not been quiet about how glad she'll be to leave this place, so I wouldn't count on changing her mind. I also see how connected Nathan is to her. So I guess I'm just saying, be careful. Again."

"Thanks for the advice," Morgan said. "And I'm trying to be careful. Again. I'm a big boy." He held Cord's warning gaze a beat longer to reinforce the point. While he knew Cord was only being a big brother, he also knew Tabitha better than he did. And somehow, in the past few days, he sensed there was more to their breakup than she was telling him.

"Look at me—I'm riding," Nathan called out, happier than Morgan had seen him in a while.

"Lookin' good, buddy," Morgan called out, turning his attention back to his son.

"He seems happy," Cord said. "Taking him out on the horse will be good for him." Then he handed Morgan the reins of the horse he'd just saddled and Morgan led it over to where the horse Tabitha would be riding stood ready. "So, you're good to go." He grinned up at Nathan astride his horse. "Looking good, cowboy," Cord said.

"I'm not a real cowboy. I'm not allowed to steer the horse myself," Nathan complained.

"You will eventually." Cord checked his stirrups, then took the rope of Nathan's horse from Tabitha.

"Why don't you mount up? I'll bring Nathan over to Morgan."

Tabitha did so but Morgan saw how she avoided looking at him. As if she also sensed his brother's disapproval of her.

She mounted up in one fluid motion, making it look graceful and easy.

Morgan got on, Cord handed him the halter rope of Nathan's horse and they were ready.

"I'll get the gate," Cord said. "You taking the ridge or going down along the creek?"

"I think we'll do the creek," Morgan said. "The terrain is less sketchy."

"See you in an hour or so?"

Morgan nodded, glancing back at Tabitha, who was looking back at his son.

"Let's go." Morgan nudged his horse, adjusting his seat as they moved along, and a peculiar happiness settled on him. The old saying "the best thing for the inside of a man is the outside of a horse" came back to him, and he smiled as they rode through the gate and out into the pasture. Hard to believe it had been years since he rode.

Tabitha came up alongside him, her eyes looking out over the valley. "This view is stunning," she said, a reverent tone in her voice.

"It is. Even more after being away from it for a while." He gave her a quick smile, then looked back at Nathan, who swayed slightly with the horse's movements, his hands planted firmly on the saddle horn. In spite of the fact that he hadn't been allowed to steer the horse himself, he was now grinning from ear to ear. "How are you doing, son?" he asked.

Nathan gave him a wary look and nodded.

"And how about you?" he asked Tabitha.

"I'm doing great." She shifted, as if getting settled in. "This saddle is fantastic."

"Should be. All our saddles were custom-made in Montana by Monty Bannister."

"Really?" Tabitha seemed impressed. "I've heard good things about his workmanship."

"Yeah, his daughter has taken over the business but it's still a going concern."

"Nothing like your own custom-built saddle. Whose was this?"

"Amber's, and before that, my mother's."

Tabitha's face grew tight, and then she looked away.

"Bad memories of my sister?" he asked, sensing her withdrawal.

She shot him a look of surprise, then shook her head. "Amber didn't pay a lot of attention to me."

"So why the tense face?"

She bit her lip, and he could see she was getting her ornery expression on.

"You don't want to talk in front of Nathan. I get it." Morgan eased out a sigh then looked out over the hills, green now from the spring rains, the halter rope from Nathan's horse slack in his hands. "Let's simply enjoy the ride, then."

"I like the sound of that." She seemed to relax and Morgan grinned at her. Their eyes met and she returned his smile. "I know I'm here because of Nathan, but I'm glad to be out riding again."

"I feel bad that we've taken you away from your work on your house." He hadn't even thought that she might have other things to do this evening. Nathan had wanted her to come, so he'd asked.

"I gladly came," she said, looking back at Nathan, who was still smiling. Still enjoying himself. "Besides, the renovations have come to a grinding halt until I can pay—" She stopped abruptly there, looking ahead again.

"Until you can pay what?"

"Doesn't matter."

He knew she wasn't going to elaborate. But that quickly reminded him of another obligation. "I'll write you a check for your work at the end of the week, if that's okay."

"I wasn't hinting at anything." She looked straight ahead.

"I know, but it reminded me of my own obligations."

"Because I'm not that broke, Morgan," she said.

"Of course you aren't." She sounded upset and he guessed he had hit a nerve.

"When are we getting to the creek?" Nathan called out.

"In a little while." Morgan drew in a long, slow breath, looking around as the setting and the rhythm of the horses' hooves eased away the tension of the past few days. The low-hanging clouds were slowly drifting away, letting beams of sun come through.

"You sound like you're getting rid of some bad vibes," Tabitha said.

A quick look over his shoulder showed him that Nathan was looking around, seeming to be off in his own world again.

"Probably am. Past few weeks have been stressful. I wish I could figure out how to connect with him."

"Taking him out like this is a good start," Tabitha said, giving him a smile. Then she too looked back as if to see if Nathan was listening. She moved her horse closer to his and lowered her voice. "I need to talk to you later. Just the two of us."

"That sounds intriguing," he said, giving her a teasing smile.

She frowned. "It's about your son."

He held her gaze a few heartbeats longer than necessary. Then he nodded, pulling himself back to the matter at hand. He had to keep his focus on his son, not be distracted by an old flame.

"I had such a fun day," Nathan said as he, Morgan and Tabitha walked into the kitchen of Morgan's house. "I liked riding horses."

"I'm glad, Nathan," Morgan said, reaching out his hand as if to ruffle his son's hair, then pulling back at the last minute, a look of pain on his features.

The gesture broke Tabitha's heart and she yearned to tell him what Nathan had said right then and there.

"But it's bedtime now, mister," Morgan said. "You need to wash up and then straight to bed."

When they'd got to the creek, Nathan said he wanted to skip rocks, so they'd ridden until they'd found a place where the creek was wider and quiet. Then the three of them had hunted up and down the creek bed looking for flat skipping stones.

By the time they'd got back on the horses, it had been getting dark. Now it was closer to 9:00 p.m. and Nathan was yawning.

"I want Tabitha to put me to bed," Nathan insisted.

Tabitha exchanged a quick glance with Morgan.

While it was touching that the boy was so attached to her, it was also growing more precarious.

What will it be like for him when I go? It's not fair to keep encouraging him.

"I think your daddy should," Tabitha said quietly but firmly.

"Can you both tuck me in?"

Tabitha knew she should go home, but she wanted to talk to Morgan about what Nathan had said to her. So she reluctantly agreed to the compromise.

While Nathan washed up, brushed his teeth and changed into his pajamas, he chattered about the ride. About skipping rocks and about cutting tree branches and floating leaves down the creek. About his horse and how fast he was and how he wanted to do it again tomorrow.

His cheeks were red and his eyes bright and Tabitha wondered if he would settle down to sleep.

"Come and see my room," Nathan said, charging ahead of both of them down the carpeted hall, his footfalls muffled.

As Tabitha stepped inside his room, the first thing she noticed was how bare it was. Nathan's bed sat along the wall under the window with a cute little desk and chair beside it. A dresser hugged the wall to her left and a shaggy rug lay on the floor.

Though a fun animal-print quilt covered the bed, no pillows lay on it. The walls were devoid of any kind of pictures or posters. No knickknacks crowded the dresser or the shelves above. No toys lay scattered on the floor or dumped in the toy box on the other side of the dresser.

She noticed the pile of cardboard boxes with his

name scribbled on them stacked in one corner of the room and guessed his personal effects were in there, hidden away.

As if he was afraid to settle down.

Tabitha thought of what Nathan had told her about Morgan and her heart melted for the little boy.

"This is my bed," Nathan announced, jumping on it and bouncing once, as if unable to contain himself.

"Why don't you get under the blankets and we can say your prayers," Morgan suggested.

"Morgan makes me say my prayers every night," Nathan told Tabitha, making it sound like he wasn't crazy about the ritual.

Oh, kiddo, you don't know how blessed you are, Tabitha thought as she stood by the foot of the bed, watching Morgan tuck Nathan in, pulling the sheets and blankets tight around him.

Her father had often been gone at bedtime, so it hadn't been unusual for Tabitha and Leanne to fall asleep in front of the television. Sometimes they'd woken up in their own bed, which meant their father had moved them during the night. Sometimes they'd woken up on the couch or on the floor, which meant he either hadn't come home or couldn't be bothered to bring them to bed.

How often Tabitha had wished her father would be home in the evenings. Just to simply be present in the house so it wouldn't feel so empty and lonely.

"May angels guard me while I close my eyes and keep me safe until I rise. Amen." Morgan finished the prayer that Nathan recited with him, a rare moment of father-son unity.

Morgan brushed his hand over Nathan's forehead

and, to Tabitha's surprise, the little boy didn't flinch away this time.

"Good night, Nathan," Tabitha said as Morgan stood.

"Can you kiss me good-night, Miss Tabitha?"

Nathan's request was spoken so quietly, Tabitha might have missed it. But it sent a shock wave through her.

"I don't… I'm not sure…" Her protests were hesitant. She didn't want to hurt his feelings, but at the same time, the boundary she thought she had set in place with this child was slowly getting eroded.

It's only a kiss and he's only a lonely, sad little boy.

It was the thought of the unpacked boxes that tugged at her emotions. So she gave in to his simple request.

But as Tabitha bent over him, inhaling the scent of toothpaste, soap and little boy, and as she brushed a gentle kiss over his forehead, a deep yearning rose up inside her.

Would she ever have a child of her own? A home of her own?

Against her will, her thoughts focused on the man beside her.

She shook them off.

"I hope you have a good sleep, Nathan," she said, brushing his damp hair back from his face with a gentle touch.

He snuggled down in the blankets looking satisfied with himself.

"Leave the door open," he said. "And the hall light on, please."

Morgan nodded, and then he and Tabitha left the room.

"Do you want a cup of coffee?" Morgan asked when they were downstairs.

Tabitha knew it was dangerous to stay. Morgan was too appealing and she was feeling vulnerable. But she needed to tell him what Nathan had said.

"Would you mind making it tea?" she asked. "I don't like to drink coffee this late."

"You're in luck," Morgan said as he plugged the kettle in. "Ella likes to drink tea as well and she gave me some different varieties, plus a teapot to boot." He pulled a large ceramic pot out of one cupboard.

"Excellent. I'm glad Ella is on top of things."

"That and more. She's a great person."

"And I understand she and Cord are engaged?"

"They'll be married in a couple of months. Probably on the ranch."

"It's a beautiful place. And the house looks nice." Tabitha walked over to the bay window of the dining room, watching the sun going down. "I imagine Cord's first wife, Lisa, did the renovations."

"After she and Cord got married. Dad had moved out already. Mom was gone, so he didn't care what Lisa changed in the house."

"That must have been hard for your father. Losing your mother and moving away from their home."

Morgan set the mugs out on the counter. "It was hard for all of us. Especially after Cord started having kids. Mom wanted to be a grandmother so badly. She was already talking about fixing up one of the rooms in the house for a nursery when Cord and Lisa got engaged. Mom was always one for looking to the future and making plans for everyone."

Tabitha knew far too well Morgan's mother's penchant for plans.

"And now you're a veterinarian and living in Cedar

Ridge again. I think your mother would have liked that," Tabitha said, choosing to be gracious. "I know you becoming a vet was important to her."

"I wish she could have been around to see it happen. She was encouraging and a support to us kids. She set high standards for us. Pushed us to achieve our potential. I really miss her."

Tabitha heard the obvious love in his voice and thought of him standing by her grave. She thought of her own mother, who, according to the doctors, had died of pneumonia when Tabitha was five. Leanne had often thought it was the constant moving and lack of money that wore her down.

What would hers and her sister Leanne's lives have been like if their mother had lived? Had she made plans for her and Leanne's future? Had she worried about what would happen to them?

Useless questions, she reminded herself.

"I'm sure you do," she said with a forced smile.

Then Morgan frowned at her as if he had just realized something. "How do you know my being a vet was important to her?"

Tabitha quickly realized her mistake and waved off his question. "Everyone knew. She always talked about you and what she wanted for your future." She walked over to the kettle, which was now boiling furiously. "Where are the tea bags?" she asked, changing the topic.

"I'll take care of that," Morgan said, opening another cupboard. As he did, his arm brushed hers, and Tabitha felt a frisson of attraction.

She knew she should leave but couldn't until she had told him about Nathan. That was the only reason she was sticking around.

Morgan made the tea. Then she took the mugs in one hand and the sugar bowl in the other.

"Let's sit in the living room." He walked ahead of her, past the dining room table, which still held some boxes as well. "I'm not completely moved in yet," he said, jerking his chin toward the table.

"Looks like Nathan isn't either." Tabitha set the mugs on the low table in front of the couch and put the sugar beside them. She settled on the couch, and then Morgan set the teapot down and sat down beside her.

"I've tried and tried to get him to unpack, but the only box he would let me open was the one with his clothes."

"It's like he doesn't want to get settled," Tabitha said.

"I wonder if it's because he thinks he might be moving back to his grandmother again. I know he's mentioned her a few times."

"It could be. Or it could be that he's afraid."

"Of what?"

Tabitha held his puzzled gaze, praying she could find the right words.

"He said something that gave me an idea of why he might be holding back from you," she said.

"Please. Tell me. I don't know what to do anymore with him." Morgan grabbed her hands as if hoping to draw out what she was going to say.

Part of her wanted to pull her hands free, but the warmth of his fingers and the way they molded around hers reminded her of better times.

How their lives had changed, she thought, looking down, tightening her fingers on his, the past melding with the present, older emotions blending with new ones.

"What did Nathan say?" Morgan encouraged, bringing her back to the present.

Tabitha hoped what he heard wouldn't be too devastating. "Please remember this was a little boy talking. That he might have gotten things wrong."

"Please," Morgan asked.

Tabitha sent up another prayer then began.

"He said his mother told him that you didn't love him," she said, keeping her voice quiet, as if that might help soften the blow. "That was why you didn't come and visit. She told Nathan that you didn't want him."

Morgan gasped.

"She said that?" His words came out in a hiss, his jaw clenched in anger.

Tabitha felt so sorry for him. To hear of such betrayal from the mother of your child had to hurt deeply. Did his ex-wife even stop to think what power she had over their child? What impact her words had?

Though Tabitha's mother died when she was only five, she still remembered things her mother had said. She still clung to the stories she'd told Tabitha. The encouragement she'd heaped on her whenever Tabitha tried to do anything.

"I'm only going by what Nathan told me," she continued. "I guess it doesn't matter how Gillian said it— what matters is that he believes it."

Morgan withdrew his hands from hers and started massaging his temples with his fingers.

"No wonder he pushes me away from him," he murmured, the devastation on his face like a knife to Tabitha's heart.

"You know it's not true that you don't love him." Tabitha placed a hand on his shoulder, trying to find a way to comfort him. "*I* know it's not true."

"So what do I do?" he asked, the pain in his voice

adding to Tabitha's pain for him. "How do I counteract what she said? How can I show him I want to be his father? That I love him."

"I think you're doing it already," Tabitha said. "You're here for him. You're finding ways to show him that every day. I'm sure, in time, he'll understand that too. You're a good father. He's so lucky to have you."

"You think so?"

"I know so. Every child should be so blessed to have a father who cares so much about their child. I wished I did."

The words came tumbling out of her mouth before she could stop them.

She read sympathy in Morgan's eyes. Then, to her surprise, he brushed his fingers gently over her cheek. "I know your father wasn't always around. I'm sure that was hard for you and your sister." His hand came to rest on her shoulder, his fingers gripping it enough to anchor her.

Tabitha's breath felt trapped in her chest as her heart jumped at his touch, the kindness in his voice and the warmth of his hand. She wanted to make a joke to lighten the moment, but her words grew jumbled. She didn't want to sound self-pitying but she wanted Morgan to understand.

"He had his moments," Tabitha said, feeling the innate need of a child to defend their parent. "He could be attentive when he wanted to."

"I remember him as a charming man."

"I'm sure your own father remembers him that way as well." Tabitha couldn't keep the bitter note out of her voice.

Morgan frowned in confusion, shifting closer. She

could see the five o'clock shadow on his chin, a faint smudge of dirt on his shirt from where he'd wiped his hands after gathering rocks. Smell the scent of soap from when he'd helped Nathan wash his face. His nearness resurrected memories of times in his truck when they talked, sitting with their arms around each other. The times they spent on the couch in his parents' house when they whispered their love for each other, keeping their voices low but enjoying the delicious thrill of being alone while his family slept upstairs.

"What do you mean by that?" he asked, his voice low, his hand still on her shoulder.

"The arena. How my dad left town with other people's money. Something I'm reminded of almost daily." Tabitha tried to pull away, but Morgan held her fast.

"You're talking about Lorn Talbot? When we bought Nathan's boots?"

"Him…and others."

"Are you talking about the money my dad put into the arena as well? Did your dad take that?"

"Not only took it, but left a number of businesses with unpaid bills."

"I heard bits and pieces about that," Morgan said. "But just from a few things Cord had said. But I never heard it from my father."

Tabitha was surprised and, somehow, was even more ashamed. The brokenness of their past and the emptiness of her future combined to create a bleakness she couldn't fight.

To her dismay, a tear trickled down her cheek. He stroked it away with his thumb.

"I don't think I've ever seen you cry before," he said.

"I'm not crying." She attempted to tamp down the upcoming tears.

To her surprise, he pulled her close, tucking her head in the crook of his neck, and Tabitha couldn't fight her emotions.

She leaned into his embrace, crying silently, promising herself this was momentary. She was lonely and tired and she appreciated his support.

"You are your own person," Morgan said, laying his cheek on her head, holding her tightly against him. "I can't think of anyone who works harder than you do. Fixing up that house, holding down two jobs, taking on extra work. I've always admired you. Even when you lived here, you always worked so hard."

"I had to," she said, resting in the sanctuary he offered.

"Because you needed the money?"

She nodded.

"Is that also why you dropped out of school?"

She was tempted to tell him the truth.

Just tell him. Let him know. Here's a chance to lay bare the secrets of the past.

Except she knew, after the admiring things he had said about his mother, after seeing him standing by her grave, grieving her loss, she just couldn't do it.

"No. That wasn't the reason," she said finally. "Though it helped me and Leanne that I could earn some money. It was always tight."

"So why did you quit school?"

She pulled back so she could look directly at him and gauge his reaction.

"I quit because at the time it was too hard for me and too much work." She saw the incredulity on his face and pushed on. "I've got dyslexia."

* * *

Morgan stared at Tabitha, incredulous.

"You're dyslexic?"

"Yeah. You know how some people say life gives you lemons? Well, it gave me melons." Her words were flippant but he heard the defensive tone in her voice as she drew away from him.

And crowding in behind his surprise was disappointment. Old feelings of lack of trust rose up. "Why didn't you tell me? We were dating. We were going to get married."

"Don't worry. I would have known where to sign my name on the marriage license," she returned, looking away.

Part of him wanted to leave it be. Tabitha was always one for keeping things to herself. Just like Gillian.

But he knew, deep down, that Tabitha wasn't like his deceased ex-wife. That unlike Gillian, she had a strong sense of pride.

She also had a growing connection with his son. Though it bothered him, he couldn't deny that she had been able to discover something he wouldn't on his own, and for that he had to be grateful.

"I didn't mean that as an accusation," he said, keeping his voice quiet.

"It sounded like one to me."

Oh, boy, was he doing this wrong. His sister often accused him of being too much of a guy and not enough of a man. Clearly the guy part of him was in action here.

"I know you don't trust me," she continued, "but that was something that I was deeply ashamed of and not ready to share. With anyone."

Her comment about his lack of trust stung even

though it was true. Yes, he hadn't trusted her when he first came back to Cedar Ridge, but he had seen a vulnerable side of Tabitha that showed him she was softer and gentler than she always came across when they were dating.

She's still leaving.

"When would you have been ready to share that with me?" he asked, bringing himself back to the topic at hand.

Tabitha drew away, wrapping her arms around her midsection. "I don't know."

"You say that I haven't trusted you and you're right, but right about now I think it goes the other way as well."

Tabitha released a humorless laugh. "I guess that could be right."

"Please. Just tell me why."

She waited a moment as if trying to decide whether or not he was worthy. He stifled a beat of annoyance but waited.

"I moved from school to school struggling with each new change, trying to adapt in so many ways. Each school was an adjustment socially and academically, which became more difficult each time," she said, looking away from him as if delving into her past. "I was never diagnosed until right before I moved here. I thought the teachers here knew but I'm guessing my records didn't get transferred. At least it seemed to me they didn't. I didn't expect to get special treatment but I thought they might understand. I had found my own coping skills. Lucky for me I had a good memory and I had a friend in Helen Jacobs, who was willing to help me out."

"Did she know?"

Tabitha nodded slowly and Morgan pushed down another beat of annoyance that he had been kept in the dark about this very important issue. "Didn't you think it would matter to me?"

"You have to understand that I was still a teenager. Still overly worried about what people thought of me. You especially. You were always the smart one. The Walsh who had everything. When you teased me when I first came to town, it hurt more than I wanted it to. And when I found out you did it because you liked me, it meant so much to me. I didn't want you to know because I was so thankful that you cared for me. A Rennie. As for school, I stumbled on as best as I could but then—" She stopped there, chewing her lip.

"Then what?"

"I was tired of fighting and working so hard. Tired of being thought dumb. And the other reality was, quitting school was a good excuse to find a job. My dad had just begun his contracting business. There wasn't a lot of money and I wanted to help out."

"What was the other reason? Was it something I said? Something I did?"

"No. Not at all. Never you." She rested her hand on his arm, her glance holding his as if pleading with him to believe her. "You were the best thing that ever happened to me."

Her words were like a double-edged sword. They confused him even as they created a flurry of hope.

"But I thought I was a waste of your time," he said. "At least that's what you told me when you broke up with me."

The words echoed between them, and as Morgan

held her gaze, he saw her determination falter and she glanced away.

"I should go."

This time, however, he wasn't going to let her avoid him. He placed his finger under her chin and turned her face to him. He knew he was taking a chance but he had to know.

"What did you mean when you said just now that I was the best thing that ever happened to you?"

Tabitha chewed her lip, as if considering what to say. "It was something I realized afterward."

"So you admit you made a mistake, breaking up with me?"

She slanted her eyes away, her lips pressed together, and Morgan felt another beat of frustration. She was still holding something back.

"Does it matter if I do? Admit I made a mistake?" she whispered.

Morgan sighed at her evasion. What they'd had was in the past. He had told himself many times that he was over her.

However, the more time he spent with her, the more questions she raised. He now sensed there was more to their breakup than what she had said to him at that time.

Though he was growing more and more determined to find out why, he also knew he had to take his time.

"It doesn't matter," he said, even though it did. "I'm glad that I wasn't simply a distraction for you."

She smiled at that but it held no humor.

"I think part of it was I was tired of feeling like I didn't measure up," she said. "Tired of feeling like I should have been more than I was, instead of less."

"You had lots going on in your life for a teenager,"

he said. "You had your father, your sister. I think it's amazing that you were able to help her out. It shows what a generous and caring person you are."

She tilted her head to one side, a quizzical expression flitting over her face. "I don't always feel so generous and caring."

"None of us do. But you have other gifts and you shouldn't sell yourself short. You've done an amazing job of fixing up your house. I can't think of too many women who would be willing and able to tackle such a big job. And I see you with Stormy. I watched you with my brother's horses and I realize that you may have problems reading words but you are amazing at reading horses."

A faint blush tinged her cheeks. "Thanks," she murmured.

"You should do more of it," he said. "Horse training. You have an amazing ability."

"I've thought of it but I need a decent place and time to do it. To do that, I need to spend my time making money so I can fix it up. And round and round we go."

"But you would consider it? If you had somewhere to train?"

"I would love to do more training."

Her simple comment gave him a glimmer of hope. Could she be convinced to stay here in Cedar Ridge?

Then she looked up at him. "Thanks again for what you said. That I have other gifts. That makes me feel better."

Morgan sensed she was getting ready to leave but he wasn't ready to let her go. He took a chance.

Cupping her face in his hands, he leaned in and brushed a gentle kiss over her lips.

He thought she might pull away, but she stayed where she was, her eyes closed, as if savoring the contact.

Then he slipped his arms around her shoulders and kissed her properly. Her gentle response kicked his heart up a notch and created an optimism he hadn't felt in years.

And when her arms went around him and she returned his embrace, when her lips softened and she melted against him, he felt as if he had finally, truly, come home.

Tabitha was the first to break the connection between them. She released a gentle sigh as she got to her feet.

Morgan stood beside her, his hand still on her shoulder. "So what happens now?" he asked.

Tabitha caught her lip between her teeth. She looked confused.

"I don't know."

Her words echoed between them in the silence of the house.

"We can't act like nothing happened because you and I both know that would be untrue."

She said nothing and Morgan was encouraged by her silence. At least she wasn't rejecting him outright.

"Will you be working with Nathan's horse again tomorrow?" he asked.

She nodded.

Morgan brushed another kiss over her cheek.

"Then we'll see you tomorrow," he whispered.

Her faint smile ignited a spark of hope. They would simply have to see how things played out. He wasn't sure how she felt, but he knew that for the first time in a long while he felt as if he had something to look forward to.

Chapter Eleven

Tabitha sat in her bedroom, legs tucked under her, Bible on her lap. She had meant to read it, but for the past hour all she had been doing was reliving that moment in Morgan's house. The kiss they had shared.

It was so familiar and yet so different. They had each dealt with so much since those first innocent moments they'd shared when they were dating.

She traced her lips with her forefinger as if to find Morgan's kiss there, then smiled at her action. She shook her head as if to dislodge the errant thoughts and looked back down at the book on her lap. She'd been reading Philippians. Today it was chapter two.

"Do nothing out of selfish ambition or vain conceit. Rather, in humility value others above yourselves, not looking to your own interests but each of you to the interests of others."

She read the words again, trying to match them with what the minister said on Sunday. About having value and worth.

Was allowing herself to think about Morgan selfish? Was she allowing her old feelings to distract her?

She set the Bible aside and looked around her bedroom. This was the first room she had fixed up in the house. It had been her and Leanne's room and they'd always hated the bright orange walls. So they'd covered them with posters they'd scrounged from thrift stores, pictures from magazines and papers from homework, making it their own.

Now the walls were a dusty blue and she used the same white trim she had in the rest of the house. Gauzy white curtains hung at the window and a blue quilt with touches of pink that she had found at a thrift shop covered the bed.

Everything she had done here was with one goal in mind. Sell the place.

But spending time with Morgan was distracting her from that. Could she allow herself that distraction? Was she being selfish?

She was thinking too much. And the cure for that, according to her father, was work.

She got up and went downstairs. And was promptly faced with her ongoing kitchen reno.

She had finally got the money that Sepp had owed her, and, to her surprise, he'd actually given her holiday pay as well. Her bills were paid for the month. When Morgan paid her, she would have enough to pay for half of her hardware-store order. Then she could finally finish the kitchen.

What happened after that?

The question hovered and for a moment she allowed herself a tiny fantasy.

She and Morgan and Nathan living in Cedar Ridge. A family.

No sooner did it form than other thoughts invaded.

Lorn's comments. Cord's reaction to her. The reality of her father's debt.

But if she finished the house and sold it, and if she and Morgan got closer…

Did she dare? Would he?

And what about Nathan? Was it fair to bring someone else into his life right now?

She closed her eyes, leaning against the opening to the kitchen.

Help me make the right decision, Lord, she prayed. *Help me not to decide for myself. Help me to make the best decision for everyone.*

"Did you get off from the clinic early again?" Tabitha asked as Morgan joined her and Nathan by the pen in her yard.

Morgan nodded, releasing a heavy sigh. Dr. Waters told him things were slower today, but he knew that wasn't true.

If it wasn't for the fact that it meant he'd be seeing Tabitha, he'd be completely disheartened.

"And how are things progressing?" he asked.

"Better," Tabitha said. "Stormy is much more willing today."

She seemed a lot more relaxed than he was. Last night he couldn't sleep. He had too much on his mind.

Tabitha's dyslexia. What Gillian had told Nathan about him not loving his own son.

You were the best thing that ever happened to me.

For so many years he had tried to come to terms with Tabitha's reasons for breaking up with him. He couldn't reconcile her telling him that she only went out with him as payback with the real true feelings he knew they had shared. And now he sensed that what she told him last night was more the truth than what she had said that horrible day.

So why did she do it?

"Nathan, Morgan, why don't you come into the pen with me," Tabitha said, her voice breaking into his thoughts. "I'd like Nathan to lead Stormy around and I'd like you to help him, Morgan."

He guessed she was trying to work on their connection as father and son, and while he appreciated it, he had his concerns. This morning, in spite of the brief moment of connection they had shared last night, Nathan had withdrawn again.

"Is that a good idea?" Morgan asked, concerned that Tabitha was pushing things too quickly with both the horse and their relationship.

"I think it is. She leads really well, and if Nathan wants to make this horse his, he has to learn to handle her sooner rather than later."

Morgan held his hands up in a gesture of concession. "Just trying to be a father," he said, trying to justify his actions.

A genuine smile curved Tabitha's lips. "I'm sorry. Just being a teacher."

Her apology and her smile combined to reignite the hope that the kiss they'd shared last night had kindled.

"And I know you're a good one," he said.

He was surprised to see a flush tinge her cheeks. "Thanks for that," she said quietly.

He shared her smile for a few beats, expectation growing, and she dragged her gaze away to focus on Nathan. Morgan got into the pen and Nathan gave him a careful smile.

One forward, two back, he told himself.

Tabitha gave Nathan some basic instructions and

handed him the halter rope. Then she walked to the opposite part of the pen and brought back a large exercise ball.

"I'm going to work on Stormy's basic curiosity to help you learn to lead her," Tabitha said to Nathan. "What I want you to do is turn your back to her, hold the halter rope and start bouncing this ball. Nice even bounces, not too high."

Nathan did as he was told and Morgan had to smile at how Stormy immediately locked in on the ball.

"Good. She's paying attention," Tabitha said. "Now I want you to walk around the pen while you bounce that ball. Morgan, you need to walk beside the horse. Not enough to distract Stormy but enough to help her know where she should go. Gentle pressure." He wondered if she was talking as much about him and Nathan as she was about him and the horse.

"This seems silly," Nathan objected, glancing at Morgan.

"It might, but wait to see what happens," Tabitha said.

Nathan started walking, bouncing the ball, and to Morgan's surprise, Stormy followed behind him, moving in rhythm with his son.

"That's a fun exercise," Morgan said, following alongside like Tabitha told him to.

"Like I said, it's working with the horse's innate curiosity." Tabitha sat on the fence, watching. Morgan tried not to be distracted by her, focusing on his son. But each time they passed her, his eyes drifted toward her and he caught her looking at him.

But she wasn't smiling.

Morgan stayed with Nathan as he walked and bounced, Stormy following right behind him, docile.

Nathan's grin almost split his face, he looked so pleased with himself.

"Look at me," he said to Morgan. "My horse is following me."

His son's joy, the fact that he actually addressed him personally, added to Morgan's own happiness. "Doing a great job, son," he called out.

When he was done she had both of them do another exercise with the ball, coaxing Nathan, encouraging him. Her patience and gentleness with his son warmed Morgan's heart. And created a faint promise of possibilities.

Him, Nathan and Tabitha? Did he dare think that far?

After half an hour Tabitha got Nathan to take Stormy's halter off and let her go out of the pen into the small pasture attached. The mare pranced around a few times, tossed her head, then came to the fence as if to say goodbye.

"I think she likes me." Nathan scrambled over the fence, joining the horse. He stroked her head, still smiling.

"I think that session went well," Morgan said as Tabitha joined them. She smiled as she looked at Nathan, still stroking Stormy's neck.

"Very well. Though it will take a lot more time before Nathan can ride her on his own, I'm feeling more optimistic."

She grinned at him, and he gave in to an impulse and stroked a loose strand of hair from her face, his fingers lingering on her cheek. To his surprise, she shifted her weight, came in closer.

He wanted to kiss her again, but Nathan was here and he didn't want to confuse his son. Things were still so precarious between him and Nathan. But now that he understood what was happening, he was willing to give him some space but, at the same time, show him that he was part of his life. That he wasn't leaving, as Nathan seemed to suspect.

"So now I have to ask you if you're free Sunday. I'm on call, but knowing Dr. Waters, he might be intercepting some of the calls anyway."

"He's not the easiest boss, is he?"

"Nope." Morgan thought about some of the things Tabitha had said. About starting his own clinic. He wasn't sure he dared to risk it. But if he didn't, he would be stuck with Dr. Waters and lousy hours for who knew how long until Dr. Waters trusted him.

"What are we doing Sunday?" Nathan asked, glancing from Morgan to Tabitha, who had now taken a few steps away, creating a distance Morgan didn't like but couldn't argue with.

"We're not sure yet," Morgan said, wary of making any plans on the fly in front of his son.

"I hope it's something fun." Then Nathan ran on ahead, skipping through the paths between the boxes and piles.

"He seems happy," Tabitha said.

"He is. I feel more relaxed now that I know better why he was so reserved around me. I feel like I can make a plan for how to treat him thanks to you."

"And how is that?"

Morgan shoved his hands in his pockets. "Just love him and be there for him. I have to get him to trust that I'm not going anywhere. Which is why not working so much for the clinic right now is a mixed blessing. It gives me a chance to connect."

"Give Dr. Waters time as well. He hasn't had someone working for him since his other partner died four years ago. He has to learn to trust too."

"I know. He did tell me that the work would be slow at first. I just hope that by the time school starts, I'll be working full-time. That's what I signed up for, after all."

"But this works out good, overall. It means you've got the whole summer to spend with Nathan."

"That's true. I'm planning a few outings with him. The zoo in Calgary. A trip to Drumheller to see the dinosaurs. Maybe a few more horseback rides." He stopped there, holding back on the idea that Tabitha might join them on the outings. He wasn't ready to move that far ahead.

"Sounds like a good plan. He's a lucky little boy."

Tabitha bent over and tugged on a piece of metal that had fallen, shifting it to a pile beside the path. She sighed as she looked over the yard.

Morgan felt again a clench of dismay for Tabitha. "This will take a lot of work to clean up," he said.

"Tell me about it," she returned, wiping her hands on her pants. "I've been tackling what I can, sorting through it, but some of the stuff is too large for me to move on my own." She shook her head at the collection of boxes and junk. "I can't believe how quickly my dad amassed all this stuff."

Morgan felt sorry for her, but as he looked around, a thought occurred to him. "I could help you clean it up."

"How?"

"I know people with trailers and tractors that have front-end loaders. In fact, I even know a guy with a backhoe that has a thumb."

"The backhoe or the owner?" she joked.

"Ha-ha. The backhoe. A thumb is an extra grapple on the bucket that helps grab stuff."

"I know what a thumb is."

Her coy smile and the way she kept looking at him

reminded him of how they had acted when they were dating. When they were both crazy about each other.

And he really wanted to kiss her again.

"I could ask them to come out and help clean this up," he said.

"Where would you bring the stuff?"

"I'd have to ask around, but I'm sure we could bring most of it to a scrap iron dealer in Calgary. Maybe one or two of the guys might want some of it."

"What could anyone possibly want?"

Morgan heard a faint note of despair in her voice as she looked around, and he gave her a quick, one-armed hug. "You never know. One man's junk is another man's treasure."

"Well, here's hoping. And thanks so much for the offer. I appreciate it. It's been a long struggle."

"You've done a lot on your own. I can't believe you haven't asked anyone for help."

Tabitha released a faint laugh. "I made a few friends the years I went to school here and since I moved back, but not the kind of friends you ask to help you out with house renovations or junk removal."

They skirted a pile of rotting lumber, following Nathan as he meandered through the stuff to where the truck was parked.

Before he joined his son, Morgan took her hands in his. "You're not on your own with this now. I'll gladly help out."

She shot a glance at Nathan, who was swiping a stick through the tall grass by the old barn. Then, to his surprise, she stood on tiptoe and brushed a quick kiss over his cheek.

"Thanks," she said. "That means a lot to me."

Morgan wanted to grab her and kiss her properly but Nathan was waving at him now.

"I should go," he said, squeezing her hand. "When will I see you again?"

"Sunday?"

"Do you want to come to my place for lunch after church? So you don't have to run the Walsh family gauntlet again?"

"Sounds good. Tell me what to bring."

"Just yourself. I'll take care of lunch."

"Okay."

"You sound like you don't trust me."

"I guess I'll have to." She grinned and Morgan felt a calm settle over the part of his soul that had always felt tense. Chaotic. Restless.

Did he dare take a leap and risk his heart again?

"You have to make sure you don't get it too close to the fire."

Tabitha knelt beside Nathan, who was trying to roast a marshmallow to golden perfection over the crackling fire Morgan had built in his backyard. So far he wasn't having much luck.

"Just keep turning it," Morgan offered, kneeling down on his other side.

"I don't know how."

Tabitha was about to show him but pulled back at the last minute. This was Morgan's job, she reminded herself. She'd been interfering too much lately and Nathan was turning to her too often.

Morgan carefully put his hands on Nathan's as he held the roasting stick, showing him how to keep the marshmallow slowly turning. Finally they were done and Morgan carefully brought the graham cracker with the piece of chocolate close and together they managed to put the whole gooey business together.

"I did it!" Nathan crowed, holding up the s'more that he and his father had made, toasted golden marshmallow oozing out the sides.

"Your dad helped," Tabitha countered.

Nathan nodded, shooting a quick glance Morgan's way and adding a shy smile. "Thanks."

Morgan patted him on the shoulder and thankfully Nathan didn't flinch away. Morgan and Tabitha exchanged a look, both of them pleased by the small step.

Nathan took a big bite out of his s'more, laughing as melted marshmallow slid all over his fingers and down his chin. Morgan pulled a wet wipe out of a bag sitting close by and handed it to his son.

"Can you wipe my face?" Nathan asked instead, holding out his chin.

Morgan obliged and Tabitha could see that even this tiny acceptance of Morgan's help was another step in the right direction.

"Well, that was a great lunch," Tabitha said, sitting back in her lawn chair and wiping her mouth with the napkin she had stuffed in the cup holder. "I haven't had hot dogs for ages."

"It was Nathan's idea," Morgan said, grinning at his son. "Not your usual Sunday lunch, but it works."

"I like wiener roasts," Nathan mumbled past a mouthful of graham cracker, marshmallow and chocolate. "Me and my mom would have them—" He stopped there, lowering his eyes as if the memory of his mother hurt.

"I imagine those were fun," Morgan said, resting his hand on Nathan's shoulder. "I think you miss having wiener roasts with Mom."

But this time Nathan pulled away. He didn't say anything but swiped the sleeve of his sweatshirt across his face, leaving a smear of chocolate on his new red hoodie.

Then, without a backward glance, he walked over to the swing set that still sat in the backyard. He got on and swung slowly back and forth, the rusty chains squeaking with every movement.

Morgan sighed and sat down on the lawn chair beside Tabitha. "I keep reminding myself that it's step by step. But sometimes those steps seem small."

"As long as he knows you love him, they'll get bigger." Tabitha wove her fingers through his and gave him an encouraging smile. "Don't forget he had a completely different relationship with his mother than you did. In spite of what she was, she was still his mother."

Morgan tightened his grip on Tabitha's hand, his other finger tracing circles over the back of her hand. "Is that how you feel about your father?"

His words ignited a tiny jolt that was a mixture of shame and affection. She wasn't sure which was uppermost.

"He was my father in spite of everything he did. But loving him was…hard at times. He and I fought a lot when I became a teenager."

"About?" Morgan prompted.

"Moving so much. Settling down in one place. Most of the time, I felt like the adult in the relationship. He was so flighty."

"It must have been hard to move here at the age you did."

Tabitha heard the regret in his voice, and before he could apologize, yet again, for how she was treated when she got here, she answered him.

"It was hard, but I didn't help matters much by being so prickly," she admitted.

"Self-defense mechanism common to self-reliant teenagers," Morgan said, his smile holding a hint of melancholy. "But it was your prickly attitude that caught my attention."

She held his gaze then grew more serious. "And it was your teasing that caught mine."

"I sometimes wonder..." Morgan let the sentence drift away as he looked back at the fire, still holding Tabitha's hand.

She wanted to ask him what he was thinking, but suddenly his cell phone rang and Nathan came over to join them.

Morgan glanced at the phone, then gave Tabitha a look of regret. "Got to take this." He answered with a hearty hello, leaning back in his chair, releasing Tabitha's hand. She guessed that was for Nathan's sake as the boy sat down beside her, swinging his legs.

"I'm not working, so I think tomorrow should work fine," he said. "Let me check." He held one hand over the phone, looking at her. "Are you around tomorrow? Owen is organizing a work crew."

Tabitha was momentarily taken aback. "Already?"

"The sooner it gets done, the better."

She had figured on working on the kitchen tomorrow. She'd planned on heading over to the hardware store to pick up whatever she could get for the money Morgan had paid her for the week.

She had tried to protest at what she saw as an overly generous amount but Morgan waved off her objections, saying that he'd asked Ernest what the going rate was for horse training and paid her accordingly.

"Okay. Monday sounds good," she said, still feeling rather uncomfortable with the idea. She knew she had to pay the people who came to help. She couldn't expect them to do it all for nothing. Owen Herne barely knew her other than the fact that she served him at the café from time to time. The other names Morgan had mentioned were familiar to her but not people she knew well enough to expect a favor from.

While she was thankful for the help, she didn't know where she was going to get the money.

"Can you help me make another s'more?" Nathan asked while Morgan returned to his phone call.

"Sure." Tabitha helped him stick a marshmallow on a stick, set out the graham crackers on the table and set a block of chocolate on it.

All the while she worked, she had half an ear on the arrangements Morgan was making on the phone. Sounded like he was getting a lot of people together.

When he was done he slipped the phone back in his pocket, giving her a self-satisfied grin.

"Why don't you look happy?" he asked.

She caught herself, forcing a smile as she turned her attention back to Nathan, who was engrossed in carefully turning his marshmallow. "I'm thrilled that the yard will get cleaned up. It's a huge job and I'm thankful that I'll be getting all that help."

"But…?"

"No. No buts. It's just…well…how many guys are coming and how much equipment are they bringing? I'm sure they can't all spare time from farming to help someone they barely know. That's a lot to ask and I'm wondering how I can…how I'll…" She faltered, wishing she knew how to say what she wanted to.

Morgan slowly nodded as if he finally understood. "You're wondering how you can pay them."

She pressed her lips together, realizing how that

sounded, but then she nodded. "That's exactly what I'm wondering."

"Tabitha. This is a community. We help each other when we can. That's what we do."

"But I can't begin to pay them back," she said. "And I don't know how."

"The books don't have to be balanced."

"In my world they do." She gave Nathan a thumbs-up when he showed her the perfectly cooked marshmallow and helped him get it on the graham cracker. Then she stood, brushing off the grass from her blue jeans, her face warm from the fire.

Morgan stood as well, his expression suddenly serious. "Well, in my world they don't. And right now that's where you are."

His words gave her heart a peculiar lift and a breathlessness she wasn't sure what to do about.

His world? Was she truly a part of his world?

Did she dare allow herself that dream again?

But, as always, then came the specter of the debt she owed. Morgan could talk all he wanted about being a part of a community and not needing books to be balanced.

But he wasn't living with the legacy she was.

A legacy of broken promises and dreams and debt that, no matter how much she wanted, needed to be repaid before she could feel free.

Chapter Twelve

The steady beeping of equipment backing up blended in the afternoon air with the shouts and orders of guys loading stuff onto trailers. A faint breeze sent clouds drifting across a blue sky and, for the first time in a long time, Tabitha felt a sense of peace and order in her life.

This morning she had been woken at 6:00 a.m. by the roar of a tractor. Morgan was driving and he was pulling a large, empty trailer. He was completely unapologetic about waking her up so early. In fact, when she had come to the door, he had dropped a kiss on her lips and called her Sleeping Beauty. Then he grinned and sauntered off to do some heavy lifting, as he called it.

Nathan had a sleepover with his cousins Paul and Suzy, so he was taken care of.

While she was getting dressed, another tractor came as well as the loader with the infamous thumb. As she stepped outside her house, two more trucks and another tractor arrived. She felt completely overwhelmed and had to fight her initial resistance to all the help. But they were here and there was nothing she could do about it now. She had to go to work at the veterinary clinic until noon. She was surprised that Morgan had asked Dr. Waters for the time off, knowing it wouldn't endear him to the man.

In the late afternoon, when she'd returned from the clinic, she was packing stuff around and trying to co-ordinate all the volunteers who had been there all day. She swallowed her pride and made a lunch run to the café. Sepp didn't say anything but thankfully made the sandwiches she needed. Even gave her a discount.

She brought them back and they were wolfed down before everyone got back to work again.

She lifted up another soggy cardboard box, holding it carefully so its contents wouldn't come out, and carried it to a flat-deck trailer that Morgan had designated for odds and ends. As she did, she looked around, still try-ing to absorb how quickly the yard was getting cleaned up and what a transformation it was.

"Hey, Tabitha," a voice called out.

Tabitha set the box down on the half-full trailer and looked around, then saw Owen Herne come striding to-ward her, waving to get her attention. Owen was tall, broad-shouldered and somewhat intimidating with his square jaw, firm lips and direct gaze. Plus he wore his sandy-blond hair long, waving over the collar of his shirt, which made him look like a Wild West outlaw. He'd been very helpful today, if a bit terse.

"Was wondering what you plan on doing with all those old cars," he said.

"Which ones?" Tabitha made a face as her eyes skimmed the yard. There were about eight to choose from.

"All of them."

She shrugged. "I don't know. Junk them?"

Owen shot her a look of pure horror, slapping a hand to his chest as if he was having heart problems.

"They're worth a ton to car collectors. Some of these are still in excellent shape. Like this one."

Tabitha looked at the car he was pointing to. Crusted with dirt, it sat up on blocks, its windshield cracked and broken, windows missing on the side.

"Seriously?"

"Dead serious." Owen scratched his chin as if thinking. "Would you consider selling them?"

"Sell them?"

"Well, I know they might mean something to you—"

"They mean nothing to me. My dad collected these from all over. Still amazes me how little time it took for him to accumulate this junk and why he thought he needed seven bathtubs."

Then she realized she was rambling, and Owen wasn't particularly interested.

"You can take them. Please," she said.

Owen slowly shook his head. "I don't like the idea of taking them. I'll bring the cars to my place and talk to my buddies. See what they might be interested in, what they're willing to pay, and take it from there."

Tabitha still couldn't absorb the idea that they might be worth something, but Owen seemed to want a reply.

"Well. Okay, then. If you don't mind taking care of it, help yourself. Please."

"Excellent." And without another word, he headed toward the flat-deck tow truck he had brought.

"So what did Owen want?" Morgan joined her, looking all sweaty and attractive with his messy hair and a streak of grease on his cheek.

"To sell my dad's cars. To his friends."

"I'm sure if anyone can, he will. Why do you look a little stunned?"

"Still surprises me that someone sees them as valuable when I've only ever seen them as junk." Then she grinned. "You're looking a little grubby," she said, lifting a corner of her shirt and wiping off the grease from his face.

He grabbed her and pulled her against him. "Just for that, I think I'm going to kiss you."

She looked around, as if checking to see who was looking.

"Everyone else is busy," he said with a laugh. "No one is paying attention to us."

Tabitha rested her hands on his shoulders, pure happiness flowing through her. "I still can't believe this is happening."

"What? The yard getting cleaned up?"

"That. But mostly this." She leaned in and kissed him, surprising herself with her boldness.

He looked surprised too. And pleased.

"I like that part too." He grew suddenly serious, his hand tucking a strand of hair behind her ear. Her heart trembled at his touch and the sight of his solemn expression, knowing what was behind it. They were cleaning up the yard to make her place more attractive to a future buyer. Hard not to avoid that reality.

Thoughts gathered up within her, confusing and contradictory. For now, she felt as if they were moving from moment to moment and she didn't dare look too far ahead.

Because every time she made plans, something changed. Every time she made a good friend, they moved. Every time something good came, life or her father's decisions or someone else's choices took it away from her.

She hardly dared hang on to this longer than the minutes in front of her.

"I better get back to work," he said, tugging at his gloves and giving her another smile.

He walked away, leaving her both confused and happy. She returned to the pile of stuff she'd been collecting and began filling a box with the glass jars she had set aside. They could go to the recycling depot. The tin cans full of screws and bolts would go in another box.

"Need a hand?"

Tabitha smiled up at Boyce, who had dragged an old metal lawn chair over to join her.

"You can give me moral support," she said, sitting back on her haunches.

"I can sort things out too." He sat on the chair that he set within reach of the pile and pulled the glass jars out, handing them to her.

"Morgan seems awful happy these days," Boyce said.

Nothing like getting directly to the point. She didn't know what to say, so she just nodded, pulling another tin can out of the pile and setting it aside.

"Happier than I've seen him in a long time," Boyce continued.

His comment hung between them, rife with expectation and question.

"I'm happier too," she said finally.

"I can see that and I'm glad," Boyce said. "You deserve some happiness in your life. So does Morgan. He told me what Nathan said to you. About his mother and what she told the boy. It was hard for Morgan to hear but it's helped him understand his son better. He wouldn't have found that out without you."

"Nathan seems to have formed an attachment to me," she said with a wry smile.

"Like father, like son."

Tabitha's face grew warm as she set another jar in the box.

"I always liked you," he added, his words making her flush even more. "Always thought it was too bad that you and Morgan broke up."

What was she supposed to say to that? *We broke up because your wife didn't like me?*

"And now you're back together again." Boyce's voice held a faint question, as if checking in with her.

She didn't reply to his unspoken query. "Together" made it sound like there was a commitment between them.

Wasn't there?

I've kissed him more than once. I'm spending more and more time with him.

Boyce sat back in the chair, giving up all pretense of helping her. "Cedar Ridge is a good place," he said, the subtext in his words not very "sub." "I think you'll find many of the people here quite forgiving."

"Some have long memories," she said, thinking back to her exchange about her father with Lorn Talbot at the shoe store. It showed her that her father's legacy was still alive and well in this town.

"You don't need to take on your dad's burdens and try to fix what he broke."

Tabitha looked down at the old tin can she held, brushing at the rust with one gloved finger. "When something is hanging over your head, it's hard to dismiss it."

"Like the money your father owes me?"

Tabitha gave him a wary look. "What do you mean?"

Boyce held her glance. "You don't have to leave because of it."

Tabitha's heart wouldn't stop pounding in her chest. She glanced toward Morgan and thought of Nathan. Thought of what Boyce had said.

Did she really want to leave?

She wasn't sure how to answer that question anymore.

"Can you turn the tap on?" Morgan asked from his position stretched out under Tabitha's sink. "I want to make sure there aren't any leaks in the water line."

When Morgan had come back from work late this afternoon, he noticed the boxes from the hardware store sitting in the back of her truck. She had picked them up yesterday, when everyone was here.

As soon as he found out they were materials to fix her kitchen, he had made plans to help her finish that. Thankfully Cord and Ella were willing to watch Nathan again.

He saw Tabitha's feet come close, heard her turn on the tap as he bit his lip, hoping, praying the line wouldn't leak.

He released a sigh of relief when all was clear.

"Looks good," he said, wriggling out from under the cabinet, almost bumping his head as he sat up. "I think we're done."

"I can't thank you enough for doing this," Tabitha

said, bending down to help him gather up the tools he'd used to install her faucets. "Made things a lot easier."

"I know you probably could have done it yourself," Morgan said, a teasing note in his voice. "But think how much time I saved you."

"I would have had to jump up and down under the sink like a rabbit, checking and double-checking everything. Would have taken me more than twice as long." She gave him a shy smile. "Thanks again."

He wanted to kiss her, but he felt grubby and wanted to clean everything, then wash up.

"Kitchen looks great," he said as he dropped the plumbing tools into the metal box, then washed his hands. "These cabinets look brand-new now that you've painted them. And the flooring is amazing. You're a woman of many talents."

Tabitha shrugged away his compliments. He knew she wasn't comfortable with them but that didn't stop him from handing them out. He sensed she could do with as much building up as he could give out.

"So, you're almost done in the house. What's next?"

"Talk to Irene Burgess. The real-estate agent. She said she had a lead on someone who might be interested." Tabitha rinsed the sink, her back still to him. "The tap works great. Thanks again for helping."

Morgan stood there a moment, torn between avoiding the topic of Irene or sticking his neck out and bringing up the future.

"So what would that mean? If you sold the place?"

Tabitha stopped moving, still not facing him, then drew in a long, slow breath. "It would mean I can finally get rid of my obligations."

"Your *father's* obligations, you mean," he clarified.

"Maybe so, but I can't act as if they're not there."

Morgan rested his hands on her shoulders, turning her to face him. "And once you get rid of those obligations?"

"I don't know what I would do. I can't work full-time for Dr. Waters, and there's not many places around here that will hire me."

"Well, what would you have done for work in another place?"

"Work at a vet clinic using my equine sciences degree as well as my vet assistant certificate. Something Dr. Waters never wanted to acknowledge."

Morgan felt a flush of sympathy for her. "Look, I know Dr. Waters is hard to deal with. I'm certainly having my own issues with him—" Morgan stopped there. He wasn't sure he was ready to talk to Tabitha about his plans yet. In spite of how things were moving between them, he still sensed a hesitancy to change her plans.

"I'm sure you could find another way to use your skills here. You could do more horse training. Horse therapy. Working with problem horses."

"I need to establish a name for myself."

"It would take time—"

"I have the wrong last name for Cedar Ridge," she said, a bitter note entering her voice.

"You could change it," he joked, trying to lighten the mood. But as soon as he spoke, he realized how she might interpret what he said.

"I'd still be Floyd Rennie's daughter," she returned. "People's memories aren't that short."

"But you're already changing people's minds. Not everyone thinks you are like your dad."

Tabitha nodded slowly, trying to absorb what he was saying.

"You're a hardworking girl," he said, hoping to encourage her. "Very unlike your father. Give Cedar Ridge another chance. It's a good place with good people. I think you can make a home here."

He stopped there. More than anything, he hoped she would take what he said to heart.

Please, Lord, he prayed. *Help her to see her own value.*

Right now, it seemed that praying was all he could do.

"So just one pill a day for the next week, and if things don't change, bring Sparkles in again." Morgan handed Mrs. Fisher the bag holding the medication and petted the calico cat on the head.

"Thanks so much, Dr. Walsh," Carmen Fisher said, scooping up her cat and cuddling her close. "And Sparkles thanks you too."

"I'm sure she does." Morgan tucked his hands into the pockets of his lab coat, smiling as his latest client walked out of the door.

"Busy afternoon." Dr. Waters joined him in the front office, bending over a computer to enter information on his most recent client as well. Then he straightened and checked the clock. "I've got to run over to the Jacobses' ranch. Check out some problems they've been having with calf scours. Mrs. Vriend will be coming in an hour or so with her dog. It needs stitches taken out. Can you deal with it?"

Morgan inwardly sighed. Really? Stitches?

"You know, Dr. Waters, I was thinking. I don't know

why you won't give Tabitha full-time work here," he said. "We could use the help."

Dr. Waters frowned and shook his head. "We're managing."

"Actually, we're not," he said, his frustration finally spilling out. "Cass is run ragged and Tabitha could use the work."

As soon as he saw the stubborn look on Dr. Waters's face, Morgan knew he had pushed too far. Maybe even made things worse for Tabitha.

"When you own your own vet clinic, maybe you'll understand what I'm dealing with," Dr. Waters snapped.

"Mrs. Vriend will have to wait," Morgan said, firmly. "I've got to go to Uncle George's place in half an hour. He needs me to see about a stallion he wants to geld and a mare that needs her teeth floated."

"That didn't show up on the roster." Dr. Waters glowered at him. All work had to be routed through Jenny the secretary, who was currently out on a quick errand.

"He called me last week. I said I would do it for him."

"I don't know about this. Can't have you taking on any job you want. We need order here."

Or complete control, Morgan thought.

"I promised Mrs. Vriend you would be available to take care of her dog," Dr. Waters continued.

"I put George's appointment into the computer." Morgan felt petty but he had to show Dr. Waters that he had followed procedure. He opened the screen to the appointments and showed his boss. "Here. I put it in Monday morning."

Dr. Waters harrumphed, then adjusted his glasses. "Okay. But you still should have run it by me."

"I thought that was why we had a secretary. To keep appointments organized."

Dr. Waters shot him another angry look and Morgan knew he had crossed yet another boundary. "I don't like being contradicted," he sputtered. "I'll call Mrs. Vriend and tell her to reschedule."

Morgan would have preferred to do that himself. Who knew what reason Dr. Waters would give her for not being able to see her dog. But he let it rest.

Dr. Waters left on another call, and when Jenny came back a couple of minutes later, Morgan was finally free to go.

As he drove away, he found himself second-guessing his decision to work for Dr. Waters. The man was getting harder and harder to deal with.

Should he go out on his own? And what about Nathan? Things were slowly, slowly getting better with him. Did he dare risk it? He wasn't much of a risk taker.

The conversation he'd had a while back with Tabitha came back to him. How she'd challenged him.

Well, maybe it was time he took a few risks. Step out on his own. Stop thinking other people had to take care of things for him. Tabitha certainly didn't wait for things to work out exactly right.

He got to Uncle George's place and drove down the hill to the ranch. A truck was racing toward him, dust billowing out from behind it. It stopped as it came alongside him, the back tires slewing sideways on the graveled driveway. Morgan recognized Devin Alexis, one of George's hired hands. The driver's window slid down.

"Didja hear?" Devin said, breathless, his hat sitting crooked on his long, dark hair. "About Tabitha's place?"

"No. What?"

"It's burning. We got the call. I'm on the volunteer fire brigade. I gotta get there. Recognized your truck coming. Thought you should know."

Then Devin spun away, spewing gravel in his haste to leave.

Morgan was frozen in his tracks, staring unseeing out the windshield of his truck as he absorbed this horrible news.

Then he made a sudden decision, reversed the truck and headed up the road, spinning his wheels as well.

Uncle George and his horses would have to wait. He needed to help Tabitha.

Chapter Thirteen

"Let me go. Please, let me go." Tabitha pushed at Owen Herne as he grabbed her arms again.

"You can't go in there. There's nothing to save," he grunted, pulling her back.

Tabitha could only stare at the flames licking at one side of the house, her heart hammering like thunder in her chest, voices screaming in her head all saying one thing.

No! No!

This couldn't be. All her work. Everything going up in smoke.

She pulled at Owen again, sobs of anger, frustration and sorrow clawing up her throat as she pulled and tugged.

"I got her."

A familiar voice. Familiar arms. Morgan was holding her tight. But she couldn't look away from her house or tear her eyes from the flames now roaring as they grew in intensity, throwing out waves of heat.

"Where's Nathan?" he asked.

"At your father's," she managed to sob. "We were

in town—" She stopped as the flames crackled loudly, growing.

"We need to step back," Morgan murmured.

Tabitha couldn't move. Her legs wouldn't obey. Everything she had done for the past few years was now being eaten up in minutes.

The firemen were finally able to pump water on the fire again, sucking water from a dugout across the road, but it was too late. Nothing could save the house now.

They heard the whinny of a horse.

"Stormy," Tabitha cried out.

"Look, someone is leading her away," Morgan said. "She'll be okay."

Tabitha was torn between the house and the horse, but it seemed that, for now, Stormy was okay.

"Everything is in there," she cried, clutching Morgan's arms, her fingers digging into his shirt. "Everything I own." Her clothes, any mementos left from her mother, the few photographs she had. The hungry flames were devouring the only precious remnants of a gypsy life as they roared and grew. She fought him once again, and then, realizing that nothing could be done or saved, she collapsed against him.

"Oh, sweetie, I'm so sorry." Morgan held her up, supporting her. He stroked her hair, then turned her head into his chest so she couldn't see the destruction of everything she owned.

Despair washed over her and the sobs she'd been holding back finally released. She clung to Morgan, her grief and sorrow washing over her in waves of torment and hopelessness. She couldn't think, couldn't process as the heat almost seared her.

Morgan drew her back, his arms holding her up as

she staggered alongside him. He fitted his arms under her legs and, ignoring her protests, scooped her up. She wrapped her arms around his neck, her face buried in his as she gave way to her grief.

She didn't know what happened after that. It was a wave of noise, bodies bustling about, the hiss of water hitting the fire and the sickening smell of smoke.

"I'm taking you to my place," Morgan said as he set her down by his truck.

"What about Stormy?"

"I'll call Cord. He can take care of her."

"But I need to stay here." Tabitha raised her head, looking past him to the fire that now engulfed her entire home, black clouds of greasy smoke roiling above the hungry flames.

"There's nothing you can do."

"I know that," she said, her hands clutching his shirt-front as she looked into his eyes, his face blurry from the tears filling hers. "But I just… I need to see it to the end."

Morgan shook his head, then gave her a tight hug. "Okay. But I'm staying with you."

"Don't you have to work?" The thought came sideways at her, a random plucking at something, anything other than the destruction of all her worldly goods.

"Doesn't matter. I need to be here. For you."

His words settled and eased some of her pain. With Morgan holding her, she watched the inferno, the heat pushing at her, her emotions drained.

Cord came with a stock trailer and Morgan helped him load the horse, but he was back right away, standing beside her.

An hour later it was over. Remnants of the brick

chimney still stood defiantly above the rubble, the hulking mass of the cast-iron woodstove in front of it, but everything else had been reduced to a blackened and smoking rubble.

"Do you think anything survived?" Tabitha asked, her voice sounding far away to her.

Morgan was quiet, which gave Tabitha her answer. No.

The fire chief, someone she didn't recognize, walked over to her. He pulled off his helmet, his face blackened by soot and streaked with sweat, then gave her a tight nod as behind him, acrid and harsh smoke still swirled and eddied, and ash and soot drifted down. "I'm so sorry we couldn't do anything. It was too late by the time we got here."

Tabitha nodded. She'd been in town when she got the desperate text from her sister.

"When did you find out?" Morgan asked, his voice pitched low, his mouth close to her head.

"Leanne texted me," Tabitha said. "She had come to the house to drop off a recipe book I had asked her for. I wanted to make a cake. To celebrate finishing the house," she said, her mind latching on to the basic, simple concept of a shared recipe. "It's a good recipe. Our mom used to make it. I gave Leanne the recipe book when she got married." She released a humorless laugh. "At least we'll still have that."

Morgan tightened his arms around her.

She wished she could tell him how much she appreciated his support. Him being there. But she was still trying to absorb what had happened.

Slowly reality washed over her like a chilly rain.

She had precious little left to sell to pay back the

debt. The acreage wouldn't be worth as much without the house. Her truck was worthless and she had no savings. Every penny she had made had been poured into the house.

Closing her eyes, she rested her head against Morgan's chest, trying to shut off the voices in her head.

"We can give you any help you might need when you deal with the insurance adjuster," the fire chief said, turning his helmet around in his hands, his expression so woebegone a bystander might suspect it was his house that had burned to the ground. "Let me know what you need."

She nodded again. Insurance. Of course. She would have to deal with them.

The thought exhausted her.

Then she eased out a heavy sigh and turned back to Morgan. "I need to go get Nathan."

"No. I'll call my dad. He'll be okay."

"Then I want to go to Leanne's place." She fished the keys out of her pocket but Morgan stopped her.

"I'll take you," he said. "You're not in any shape to drive."

"I can go."

Then Morgan gently but firmly extricated the keys from her tight grip. "I'll drive you," he said.

Another sob broke free and again she was leaning against Morgan. "I'm sorry. This is so silly. It's just a house. Just stuff."

Morgan smoothed his hand over her hair, rocking her lightly. "Maybe, but it was yours. It represents a lot of hard work."

Hard work. Work to make the house sellable. Work that had just gone up in flames.

A colossal waste of time.

Morgan talked to Owen about picking him up from the Walsh place and Morgan led Tabitha back to her truck. He helped her into the passenger side and, as he got in, Tabitha saw it through his eyes. Torn seats, knobs missing on the dashboard. Visor tied with hay wire.

A broken-down truck for a broken-down life.

Tabitha closed her eyes, trying to shut off the chattering in her brain.

The drive back to her sister's place was silent. Tabitha didn't know what to say and Morgan was quiet too. But he had his hand on hers all the way there. She clung to him, thankful for his presence and for his strength.

All she wanted to do was crawl into a bed, pull the covers over her head and sink into denial even though she knew the sight of her house burning would be seared into her memory. She knew she would constantly relive it and behind all that would be the growing despair that now she had nothing to use to pay off her father's debts.

Finally they were at Leanne's place.

Leanne was at the front door and coming toward them as soon as Morgan shut the engine off.

She pulled open the truck door and grabbed Tabitha's hand.

"Oh, hon. I'm so sorry." The anguish in her sister's voice was almost her undoing.

"It's not like someone died," she said, trying to put her own wavering emotions in perspective.

"No. But still, it's a huge loss."

And Leanne would know what was at stake.

She let her sister help her out of the truck and then Morgan was beside her on the other side. "I'm not an invalid," she protested.

Morgan said nothing as he slipped his arm around her shoulders. They walked up the stone sidewalk and then up the wide stone stairs leading to double doors flanked by tall narrow windows, with a large, half-round window arched over the entire entrance.

For the briefest moment Tabitha felt a flash of envy at the impressive house that her sister called home.

Leanne led her through the echoing front foyer with its sweeping staircase to a narrow hall leading to a breakfast nook off the kitchen.

"Sit down, hon. I'll make you a cup of tea. Morgan, can I get you anything?"

Morgan hovered and Tabitha could see he wasn't sure what he should do.

She looked up at him, giving him a careful smile. "I'll be fine. I'm with my sister."

He laid his hand on her shoulder. "Are you sure? I can stay."

"No. I'm sure you have work to do, and the last thing you want is to antagonize Dr. Waters."

"Actually, I'm supposed to be right here, so I'll go find George, get the work done. Then I'll be back."

"There's no need," Tabitha said even though the thought that he would be right on the yard gave her some comfort.

"I'll be back." He bent over and gave her a gentle kiss on her forehead, then left.

Tabitha leaned back in the chair as her sister bustled around the kitchen. "Where's Austin?"

"Sleeping. I put him to bed as soon as I came back from your place." Leanne gave her a look of despair. "I wish I had gone sooner. Maybe—"

"Stop. Don't think that. Maybe you'd have been

caught in the house." She had to stop her mind from going there.

"I just came there and I saw the flames." Leanne sat down beside Tabitha and grabbed her sister's hand. "I didn't know what to do. I called the fire department, then you. Then raced back here to see if the hired hands could help out."

"You did the right thing. You couldn't have done anything more." Tabitha rolled her head to ease the crick of tension in her neck. Then she took a long, slow breath. "Well, I guess I'll have to change my plans now."

Leanne squeezed her hand. "No matter what happens, you know you're not alone. I'm here. I'll be praying for you. And now it looks to me like you've got Morgan beside you."

Tabitha eased out a smile. "Yes. I guess I do."

But even as she held that thought came a harsher reality.

Now she had no way of paying back the people her father owed. Especially Morgan's father.

Morgan finished filing down the horse's teeth, listening halfheartedly to Uncle George's chitchat about the upcoming rodeo this summer, the rest of his mind on Tabitha. He wanted to go see her but also realized that being with her sister was probably exactly what she needed.

"Sad what happened to Tabitha," George was saying now. "Those Rennie girls haven't had an easy life. I know Leanne hasn't."

Morgan didn't know how to respond, so he nodded as he popped off the eye protection he'd been wearing, wrinkling his nose at the smell of filed horse teeth. He'd done this a few times in his previous practice and still wasn't used to the acrid scent.

He removed the speculum and put it in a plastic bag to sterilize at the clinic, then stroked the horse's neck to reassure it. The horse blinked slowly, still under the effects of the mild anesthetic Morgan had given him to keep him calm during the procedure.

"He should be eating much better now that I've gotten rid of those hooks on his teeth," he said to his uncle, picking up the tools he'd been working with and putting them away in the veterinary kit.

"That's good. He'd been spilling his grain and chewing on the fence. Figured something was up." Uncle George untied the halter and cross tie they'd used to keep the animal still. He gave the horse one final pat, then followed Morgan to his truck. "So, is there anything left of Tabitha's house?"

Morgan shook his head. "Just a brick chimney and what looked like a heavy-duty cast-iron woodstove."

"Really? Chimney fire from the woodstove, you think?"

"It's summertime, so I doubt it. Doesn't matter anyway. Everything else is gone." Another wave of sorrow and frustration for Tabitha swept over him. And if he felt like this, he couldn't imagine what she was dealing with.

"In a way, I'm not surprised. If a Rennie is involved it can't be good."

"How can you say that? Your own daughter-in-law is a Rennie."

"I didn't have any choice in that. But she gave me a grandson. Someone to carry on the Walsh name. And for that I'm grateful." George's expression grew serious and Morgan thought of his cousin Dirk, who had been married to Leanne. Dirk had died in a tragic vehicle accident. He knew it was hard on his uncle. "But she's a good girl in spite of her father," George said in a condescending tone.

"Tabitha is a good girl too," Morgan said. "She's a hard worker and she's determined to do right. To make up for what her dad did."

"That won't happen now," Uncle George said with a snort, his eyes narrowing and his fists clenching. "Floyd Rennie was a snake who cheated a lot of people."

Morgan stopped there, knowing that anything he said would only get his uncle riled up. He wanted to see Tabitha, not listen to yet another one of Uncle George's rants.

"So is that everything?" Morgan asked, slamming the tailgate of his truck shut, shifting the conversation.

"In a week or so I'm going to need you to come and look over a couple of my mares. Can't seem to get them bred."

Morgan pulled out his phone and made a quick note. "Seem to be getting more horse work lately," he said as he shoved his phone back in his pocket.

"Yeah. More people getting acreages closer to town too. They all want horses and Dr. Waters can't keep up." George shook his head in disgust and Morgan sensed another rant coming.

"Thanks for the work," he said to his uncle. "I want to see how Tabitha is doing. Then I should push off."

"Sure. And I'll call Doc Waters. Tell him I want you to come to take care of the horses."

Morgan didn't know how that would go over with his prickly boss, but he let it be. That was to deal with at another time.

He drove to the house and parked his truck in the driveway.

He had seen Uncle George's place many times when he and his brother would come to play with their cousins, Reuben and Dirk, but it always made him shake his head. His dad often teased his uncle about his need to impress, and this house, with its soaring roofs, brickwork and timbered entrance, did all that and more.

He rang the doorbell and stepped inside. Leanne came to the front entrance, then stopped when she saw him.

"Is Tabitha okay?" he asked, pulling off his hat and turning it around in his hands.

"She's sleeping, believe it or not." Leanne slowly shook her head as if trying to absorb what had happened. "Poor girl is exhausted."

"I believe it." He gave her a rueful smile. "Tell her I said hi. I'll stop by tonight, when I'm done with work, if that's okay."

"I'll ask her when she wakes up."

Morgan didn't miss the switch in her words and wondered what she meant by it.

"Okay. Can you ask her to call me?"

"I can do that." Leanne crossed her arms over her chest in a defensive gesture, which annoyed him. As if she had to defend Tabitha from the big bad Walsh.

He dropped his hat back on his head and left. Nothing more to do until Tabitha called.

He just hoped she would.

Morgan's phone rang and he yanked it out of his pocket, then frowned at the unfamiliar number on the display. Someone calling from Idaho? He was about to ignore it, thinking it was a telemarketer, when the number registered. Nathan's grandmother.

"Hey, Donna," he said as he tucked the phone under his ear. He dumped a handful of pasta into the water he had boiling on the stove, glancing over at Nathan, who was playing some computer game on the television. When he went to his dad's place, he had offered supper, but Morgan wanted to be available in case Tabitha called.

But she hadn't.

"Is this a bad time?" Donna asked.

"No. Not at all. How are you?"

Donna sighed, and he heard loneliness and sorrow. "I'm okay. Surviving."

Morgan felt a flush of guilt. He should have called sooner to see how she was doing. She had lost her daughter, after all, and was living hundreds of miles away from her grandson.

"I'm sure it's been difficult."

"I'm coping. How is Nathan doing?" she asked. "He must be loving it on the ranch."

"He's coping too," Morgan said. "Did you want to talk to him?"

"In a minute. I wanted to double-check on the arrangements you had made for my birthday. If you were driving down or flying."

Driving? Flying?

Morgan scrambled through his brain, thinking. Then it hit him like a ton of bricks. Of course. He had promised Donna that he would bring Nathan to visit her on her fiftieth birthday. She was throwing a huge party and she wanted Nathan to be there.

"Don't tell me you've forgotten," she said, a hurt tone entering her voice.

"I'm sorry," he admitted. "Things have been haywire since I got here." Seeing Tabitha and getting involved with her had erased Gillian from his mind. "I don't have my calendar handy but is it next week?"

"No. This Friday. I was hoping you could come early. Give me some time to spend with Nathan before things get busy."

That meant he would have to drive, which meant they had to leave tomorrow morning. It was at least nine hours from here to Coeur d'Alene, where she lived. How could he have been so dumb to forget this?

But even worse, it meant leaving Tabitha on her own for a few days right at this horrible time. He stifled a groan at the timing and at his forgetfulness.

"We'll be there tomorrow night," he said with more assurance than he felt. He'd have to ask Dr. Waters for more time off and he was fairly sure how that would go over. Not well.

Suddenly, however, he didn't care. There were bigger things going on in his life right now than dealing with a finicky, unpredictable boss.

"I'm so glad. I'm looking forward to seeing Nathan again."

They chatted about Nathan and Stormy. Morgan had never got to know Donna, so the conversation didn't last that long. They said goodbye, and when she ended the call, Morgan dropped his phone and leaned back on the counter.

What lousy timing.

Then he felt horrible for the resentment he felt. Donna

had every right to see her own grandson on such a milestone birthday.

But why did it have to happen now?

Oh, Lord, he prayed. *I want to be here for Tabitha. I want to support her. But I want to do right by my son.*

He knew the prayer wouldn't change anything, but he needed to vent and let go of his frustration.

He grabbed the phone and for the umpteenth time he dialed Tabitha's number.

And for the umpteenth time it went directly to voice mail. She must have shut her phone off. This time, however, he left a message.

"Hey, Tabitha, I forgot about Nathan's grandmother's birthday. We have to leave tomorrow for Idaho. I'll try to call again when we're on the road. Please call me back." He paused, wanting to say so much more, but there was no way he was doing that on a voice mail. "Thinking of you and praying for you," he said instead.

Then he ended the call and did exactly that.

Chapter Fourteen

"We can't say much until the insurance adjuster files his final report," Carl Tkachuk said, his hands folded on the desk, his expression suitably sympathetic. "Lucky for you he's able to come tomorrow, which is lightning quick. I pushed him to get it done."

Tabitha shifted on her seat in the insurance office, struggling to make sense of what Carl was saying. "I appreciate that," Tabitha said, clutching her backpack, the only thing she had left that belonged to her.

"For now, all I can give you is out-of-pocket expenses. To cover a hotel and meals for you."

"I understand." Tabitha was still walking around in a haze, trying to process what had happened.

While Carl talked about the process of filing a claim and what would happen, her mind drifted off.

She'd lost everything. Clothes. Shoes. Groceries. The tiles she needed to install above the new counter she'd put in. The few pictures she had of her mother. A few school mementos, like the notes she and Morgan would shove in each other's lockers in high school. Silly little messages about how much they missed each other.

The thought of Morgan sent another sob creeping up her throat.

Deal with what is right in front of you, she told herself. *Don't think too far ahead.*

Behind that came another desperate prayer. One of many she'd been winging heavenward the past twenty-four hours.

Please, Lord, give me the strength to get through this.

Yesterday, after she had woken up from an exhausted sleep, she had lain in the bed at Leanne's house fighting a myriad of emotions. Grief, anger with God that He had let her down, a very unwelcome jealousy of her sister and the beautiful house she lived in.

But more than that was a deep, unwelcome and all-too-familiar sorrow and shame.

How could she face Morgan now? As long as she could cling to the hope of paying back his father, she dared dream of a future with him. The dirty slate her father had left could be wiped clean. The books balanced.

She had dared to make tentative plans to maybe stay in Cedar Ridge. To see if she could, somehow, somewhere, set up a horse training facility. To allow herself the faintest dreams of a life with Morgan. With Nathan.

But now?

Now Morgan was gone along with her tentative hopes. He had left a message on her phone but she hadn't called him back. She couldn't. Not yet.

Too many things going on in my head. Deal with them one at a time.

"I do have one question, though," Carl was saying.

Tabitha snapped back to the present and gave him a tentative smile.

"Sure," she replied.

He rolled his pen between his fingers. "I was chatting with the fire chief. He told me that all that was left of the house was a brick chimney and what looked like a woodstove."

"Yes. My dad put it in. Said he liked wood heat."

"Were you using it?" He made a quick note on his file. His deepening frown created a tiny foreboding of dread.

"No. It was a hassle. I never used it."

"So you didn't have it going yesterday?" Another note, a pursing of his lips and Tabitha's apprehension grew.

"Of course not. It's summer. No." She felt a niggling suspicion that they might pin the blame for her house burning down on a chimney fire.

Carl tapped his pen on the folder, then flipped through another file, folded papers back, scratched his temple with his pen, whistling through his teeth while he read. Then he sat back in his chair, his fingers drumming on the desk.

"So here's the thing. Your policy doesn't have coverage for a woodstove."

"But it's the same policy my dad had. On the same house and I never used the stove."

"I realize that, but for all practical purposes, you taking it out makes it a new policy. We don't grandfather in clauses in insurance policies. They are based on each person as an individual. Your father may have had a woodstove in his policy on the house, but you don't."

A shiver of dread trickled down her spine. "I was told I could take over my father's policy."

Carl slowly shook his head, trying to look sympathetic but not hitting the mark. "Whoever told you that was wrong. You are a new and unproven client— it would be a new policy. They would have given it to you to read over if you had questions."

Tabitha remembered now. The lady who had sold it to her had given her exactly that opportunity, but Tabitha hadn't wanted to sit in her office, struggling to decipher the words of an insurance document in front of a lady who had already treated her with vague disdain and a measure of impatience. It was difficult enough to work her way through books or newspaper stories, let alone the convoluted legalese of an insurance policy.

"I'd asked questions about it," she said. "Lots of questions. But how…? Why didn't…? Why wasn't I told about the stove? Whoever drew it up should have known what my dad's policy covered. Why didn't they inform me about the woodstove? I would have removed it." She was growing more frantic, more angry, more frustrated and, as a result, more shrill. She clamped her lips together as she caught Carl's expression.

"I'm sorry. We'll have to see what the adjuster says, of course, but I have to warn you—it doesn't look good."

Don't cry. Don't give him the satisfaction.

Oh, Lord. Why all this too?

Had she done something horribly wrong somewhere? Messed up so badly that she was being punished?

I should have read the policy. I should have checked it over.

Trouble was, she couldn't.

Another reminder of who she was and what she couldn't do.

Illiterate, dyslexic Tabitha.

Behind that came an even more insidious thought.

She was glad Morgan was gone so she didn't have to face him with yet another failure in her life.

Morgan hit a button on the screen on his truck's dashboard, ending the phone call he had tried to make to Tabitha. Again.

Nathan was sleeping in the backseat of the truck, his head lolling sideways despite the pillow Donna had provided for the trip back to Cedar Ridge.

The visit with Donna had gone well. She was so excited to see her grandson but, to Morgan's surprise, Nathan had acted shy around her. Morgan had felt bad for Donna, but what had shocked him even more was how Nathan had clung to his hand.

In spite of the small breakthrough he'd experienced with Nathan, however, the entire time he was gone, his thoughts were tied up with Tabitha.

In spite of a number of calls from him to her, she had neither answered nor called him back. He was trying not to panic. Too easily came the memory of the last time she had walked out on him. How she had shut him out and he hadn't heard from her again.

Please, Lord, get her to answer my calls, he prayed.

His mother had always told him when he prayed to be specific. Well, he was being specific now.

An hour later, he pulled into his own driveway, parked the truck and dragged his hands over his weary face. His ears were ringing from the steady engine noise and his head ached.

Nathan still slept while Morgan took their suitcases into the house. When he came back, he unbuckled his son and smoothed his hair back from his face. Nathan's lips twitched, and when he opened his eyes and looked at Morgan, he smiled.

Morgan's heart clenched at the sight, and as he lifted the still-sleepy boy out of his booster seat, Nathan wrapped his arms around Morgan's neck, laying his head on his shoulder.

Morgan laid his head against his son's, a deep, abiding love seeping through his soul as he held his boy tight. He carried him up the stairs into the house, his booted feet echoing in the silence. He brought him upstairs and laid him on the bed, tugging off the boy's boots. Nathan murmured a protest, and then his eyes opened and he smiled at Morgan.

"Are we home?"

"Yes. We are."

Nathan looked around. "Where's Tabitha?"

He was surprised that his son expected Tabitha to be here.

"She's not here."

"But she doesn't have a house anymore. Because it burned down. She should stay here."

At one time Morgan had allowed himself the dream that this might be what happened, but that was not how things seemed to be playing out.

"She has a sister, Leanne. She's staying at her place."

Nathan didn't seem satisfied by that answer. "Can we go see her?"

"Not tonight," Morgan said, not sure when that might happen given Tabitha's lack of contact with him.

"Tomorrow?"

"We'll see."

Nathan seemed satisfied with that and allowed Morgan to change him into his pajamas. He snuggled down in his bed and smiled as Morgan settled on the edge of his bed to say good-night.

"I'm glad we could see Gramma," he said.

"I'm glad too." Morgan brushed the boy's hair away from his face again, just because it gave him a chance to touch his son, to connect with him.

"But I like being home." Then Nathan looked around his room. "Can I hang up my posters tomorrow?"

"Of course you can," he said, smiling so hard it almost hurt. "We'll put them up first thing in the morning."

"Gramma never let me hang up my pictures. She always said I would have to take them down again. But she told me that I was staying here. Forever. And that you would take care of me." Nathan's eyes seemed to bore into Morgan's. "You will, won't you?"

"I will. Forever and ever." Then Morgan took another risk, bent over and kissed his son's forehead. "I love you, Nathan."

Nathan grinned, then pulled the blanket up around his neck and curled up on his side. "I love you too."

Morgan thought his heart would burst with joy. Though he had been extremely reluctant to visit Donna, something good had come from the visit after all.

He gave Nathan another kiss and said his prayers with him. He didn't want to leave but his cell phone started buzzing.

He felt a jolt of anticipation. Tabitha?

He pulled the phone out of his pocket as he left the room, leaving the door open and the hallway light on exactly the way Nathan liked it.

But his heart dropped as he saw the number on the screen.

Not Tabitha.

His brother, Cord. Probably calling to make sure he made it home okay. Morgan was tired and didn't feel like talking to anyone, so he slipped the still-ringing phone back in his pocket and made his way downstairs. He sank into his chair and dropped his head on the back, staring up at the ceiling.

So, now what?

He felt as if his life had been thrown off course the past few days. The plans he had dared make for a future with Tabitha seemed even further from becoming reality than ever.

And if Tabitha wasn't answering his calls, he doubted she would be coming to take care of Nathan.

Chapter Fifteen

"What are you doing?"

Leanne walked into the spare bedroom and sat down on the chair tucked into the corner.

Tabitha shoved the few clothes her sister had given her into her backpack and zipped it shut, trying not to wince at how little space the few earthly possessions she had took up.

"I need to get away. Just leave for a few days."

"Where?"

"I'm heading up to Sundre. I have an old college friend there." Tabitha slung her backpack over her shoulder and gave her sister a wan smile. "I'll be back in a couple of days."

Leanne held her gaze, her expression serious.

"Have you talked to Morgan?"

"I phoned Ella and told her that I need to get away. She offered to take care of Nathan."

"That's not what I asked." Leanne blew out a sigh and got up. Tabitha tensed herself for the mini-lecture she guessed was coming. She so didn't want to talk about Morgan. Didn't want to think about the failure her life had become, yet again.

"He's been trying to get hold of you. I think you should at least let him know you're okay."

"Well, I'm *not* okay." Tabitha lifted her head, chin up, gaze holding Leanne's. "I've got no way to pay back his father. I couldn't even take the time to read my insurance policy because it was too much work and as a result I messed up. I'm a—"

"Don't you dare say it." Leanne held up a finger in warning like she would to her toddler son. "You did what you were supposed to do. Your insurance adviser should have done exactly that. Advised. It wasn't your fault."

"Well, you can say that all you want, but at the end of the day I still don't have a house to sell."

"You have the land. It's got to be worth something."

Tabitha shrugged. "Not as much as the house." She blew out a sigh, wishing her sister would let her go. "Anyhow, I need to get away and clear my head."

"I wish you would let me help," Leanne said.

As soon as Leanne had found out about their father's debt, she had tried to give Tabitha money as well, but Tabitha had refused. Though Leanne worked on her father-in-law's ranch, George only paid her enough for her day-to-day expenses. Tabitha knew Leanne didn't have much extra money. Besides, if she did have extra, Tabitha preferred that her sister set it aside for her son.

"I'll figure something out," Tabitha said with a weary smile.

"You'll call me, though?" Leanne asked.

"Of course I will."

"And Morgan?"

Tabitha answered that with a shrug. She wasn't ready to face him yet. Didn't know if she ever would be.

I can't avoid him forever and I still have an obligation to Nathan.

The thought of leaving him, abandoning him, bothered her more than she wanted to think about. But seeing Nathan meant seeing Morgan, and there was no way she could face him right now.

"I'll call you when I get to Sundre," Tabitha said, giving her sister a quick hug. "Give Austin a kiss for me too."

Leanne returned her hug, then held her by the shoulders, looking like she wanted to say more, but then she shook her head. "I will. Drive safe and call me when you get there."

Tabitha nodded. Then, before she could chicken out, she left. As she got in her truck and drove away, she tamped down her second thoughts. What she didn't tell her sister was that she wasn't going to Sundre only for a break.

She was going for a job interview, and if she got it she was leaving Cedar Ridge and all the bad memories behind her. Starting fresh in a new place as she had hoped. She would sell the acreage and give what she could to Boyce and not come back.

Her sister's question about Morgan rang through her head. Leanne seemed to expect that she would simply call up Morgan and carry on. But she knew that wasn't happening. She was too ashamed.

It was the For Sale sign that finally did it.

All week Morgan had been waiting to hear from Tabitha. Dr. Waters was grumbling about her taking time off. He would have more things to grumble about if things went the way Morgan hoped.

Nathan had been upset as well, and there were times that he wasn't sure which betrayal bothered him more. Her betrayal to his son or to him.

Morgan had thought that something was happening between him and Tabitha. Some relationship that meant that she would turn to him if she needed help, but clearly he had read it all wrong.

Nathan was at his father's place, so when he was done working, he drove to Leanne's. He needed some answers.

Tabitha's sister was working in the garden when he pulled in.

He got out of the truck, then hesitated, feeling a sudden attack of nerves. Did he truly want to hear what she might have to say? What if Leanne told him that Tabitha was never coming back?

Please, Lord, show me what to do, he prayed. *Help me to say the right words. Ask the right questions.*

Leanne's little boy, Austin, was waving a stick around, chasing butterflies. Leanne was bent over a row of beans, weeding them, humming to herself. Okay. This was good. Tabitha's sister was in a good mood.

Morgan sent up another prayer, straightened his shoulders and marched toward the garden.

Austin was the first to see him. He stopped, then ran to his mother, crying.

Excellent start, Morgan thought, stopping where he was, concerned he would make the poor kid even more afraid.

Leanne caught him just as she looked over her shoulder. She lifted Austin into her arms, then stood.

"Hey, Morgan."

Morgan drew in a long, slow breath, then walked toward her. "Hey, Leanne. I'm hoping you can help me."

Leanne squinted against the sun, her expression unreadable. "Let's sit over there," she said, pointing her chin in the direction of the patio and the wicker furniture parked in the shade of a large second-story deck.

Leanne set Austin down by a box of toys and he immediately began rummaging through it.

"I imagine you're here to ask me about Tabitha," Leanne said as she sat down.

Morgan decided to go directly to the point. "I noticed there's a For Sale sign on the property."

"Yes. I tried to talk her out of it. Tried to tell her to work with the insurance company and rebuild but—" Leanne stopped there, cutting her gaze over to Austin.

"But what?" Morgan sensed there was more going on.

"Not my story to tell."

"Well, don't try to tell me to call Tabitha to find out because she's not returning my calls."

"Still?"

Morgan nodded. Leanne sighed.

"What's going on, Leanne?" he pressed. "Please tell me."

Leanne looked as if she still wasn't sure what to say.

"I care about your sister. I really do. She means as much to me as my son does. I know when I first moved back here I wasn't the kindest to her, but I had my reasons."

"It was because she broke up with you."

"Yes, and did what she's doing right now. Retreating and shutting me out. She didn't tell me why she left then and she won't tell me now."

Leanne folded her arms over her chest, looking out over the backyard, a wistful expression on her face. "I'm sure that was a hard time for you."

"Hard? I had bought an engagement ring."

"I know. Tabitha told me. It broke her heart to walk away from you."

"I don't want to go back over the past," Morgan grumbled. "That's finished. I need to deal with the present."

"Have you ever thought the past and present might be connected?"

"What do you mean?"

"When Tabitha left you the first time, did you ever wonder why she made such a huge change?" Leanne said. "I mean, one minute you guys were planning a future together. The next, she'd left town."

"She told me that I'd meant nothing to her. That she'd been leading me on." He couldn't keep the bitter tone out of his voice.

"And you believed her?"

"I tried to challenge her about it but she got angry and started yelling at me, told me that I was a fool to think that I meant anything to her. Then she left and I heard nothing from her. The next time I see her she almost runs over my kid."

"I heard that Nathan came out of nowhere," Leanne said, a slightly annoyed tone in her voice. "It wasn't her fault."

Morgan smiled at her dogged defense of Tabitha.

"At any rate, it'd been a long time of nothing," Morgan said, returning to the topic at hand. "And it looks like she's descending into the same pattern and I don't know what to do."

A moment of silence fell over the conversation. Then Austin fell and started crying. Leanne hurried over to pick him up, then brought him back, holding him close. She kissed his head and sat down, still cuddling him.

The sight made Morgan feel despondent.

"He's a lucky boy," Morgan said.

"In one way, yes. In another, no."

"What do you mean?"

"He doesn't know his father."

"Of course. I'm sorry."

"But he has me. And a mother will do whatever she needs to do to take care of her child. Just like your mother did."

Her words caught his attention. "What do you mean? What did my mother do?"

Leanne held his gaze another beat. Then when Austin wiggled off her lap, she leaned back in her chair, crossed her arms over her chest and stared over the backyard. "Ask Tabitha."

"And how am I supposed to do that?"

"Go. Find her. Ask her. You let her go once without challenging her. Without trying to find out why she did what she did." Leanne reached up and toyed with a strand of her hair, twirling it around her finger. "Sometimes a girl likes to know that you're willing to go the extra mile. To fight for her. Take a risk." Then she looked over at him. "In spite of how you see it, I don't think you did that the first time."

Morgan could only stare at her.

"You don't know what she said to me. You can't understand how humiliating it was for me."

Leanne snorted. "Don't talk to a Rennie about being humiliated. If you care about her like you claim you do, you'll know what to do." She got up and picked up her son. "Now if you'll excuse me, I have a garden to weed."

Morgan got up as she left, more puzzled than ever. He still couldn't figure it all out, but there was one thing he did know. Leanne was right. He needed to forget about himself. His pride and his hurt feelings.

He needed to fight for the girl he cared about. He had let her walk away from him once before without chasing after her. He wasn't going to let it happen again.

Chapter Sixteen

Tabitha dropped her backpack on the bed of the motel and pressed the heels of her hand to her face. Another round of interviews in yet another town and still no job. She had come to Sundre with such high hopes but her spotty résumé was no help.

She sat down on the bed and flicked through her cell phone. Thankfully Morgan had stopped texting her and leaving messages. She didn't listen to any of them. She was afraid they would make her cry, and she was tired of crying and feeling weak.

She closed her eyes, the headache hovering behind her eyes threatening to explode.

I've been through worse, she reminded herself, remembering other motels, waiting with Leanne for her father, wondering when he would show up.

Her thoughts shifted to Nathan, and she felt another clench of dismay.

Probably just as well she left, she told herself. *Morgan is his father and that's all he needs.*

She took a breath, then pulled out her Bible and

opened it to a passage she'd been reading last night, the same one the pastor had preached on a few weeks ago.

"Are not five sparrows sold for two pennies? Yet not one of them is forgotten by God. Indeed, the very hairs of your head are all numbered. Don't be afraid—you are worth more than many sparrows."

Each time she read this she was reminded of her worth. Self-worth had been something she'd struggled with so much of her life. Even now, in spite of what she read, it still was difficult to accept her true value.

Her rumbling stomach reminded her it was time to eat. Though she had told her sister she was staying at her friend's, it hadn't worked out, so Tabitha opted instead to stay at a motel, renting a kitchenette to save a few dollars.

She put her Bible down and got up to make something when a knock on the door stopped her in her tracks.

Who would be coming here? Her friend was working. No one else in Sundre knew she was here.

Then her heart jumped. Maybe it was one of the employers where she had dropped off a résumé. Come to give her a job?

Even as she hurried to the door, her practical self told her not to be silly, but she couldn't stop a sense of expectation.

Then she opened the door and the expectation turned to utter shock.

Morgan stood in the doorway, his cowboy hat in his hand, his expression guarded and weary. His eyes sought her out, an almost hungry look in them that set her heart racing.

"What…? How…?"

"Leanne" was his concise reply.

"I asked her to not tell you."

"Why not?"

She wasn't sure what to say.

"Aren't you going to invite me in?" he asked.

Tabitha looked over her shoulder at the cramped motel room, the dinginess of it hitting her suddenly.

"No."

"I need to talk to you. Can we find another place?"

She hesitated, not sure she wanted to talk to Morgan yet or what to make of his presence here. She had thought of him so much, and seeing him now, his hair pressed down from his cowboy hat, the stubble shading his jaw giving him a weary and vulnerable look, she would have a hard time saying no.

"I'm not leaving until we talk, Tabitha. Until you explain to me why you left. *Both times.*"

He emphasized the last two words, which sounded ominous to her.

Confusion and fear warred with a surprising happiness at seeing him again.

"I'm not letting you walk away again without the truth," Morgan said.

She sighed as she heard the resolve in his voice.

"Okay. I'll get my key," she said, stepping into the motel room and closing the door on him. She stood in the middle of the room, her heart pounding in her chest.

Help me, Lord was all she could say as she pulled the key to her room out of her backpack and shoved it into her pocket. She stepped outside, then turned to face Morgan and his questions. But before she would answer any of his, she had her own.

"How's Nathan?"

"He's good. Asking after you."

She fought down a sense of disappointment in herself.

"And Stormy?"

"Not asking after you."

She almost smiled at that. "Why are you here?"

"I told you. I need answers."

That didn't sound very romantic. But she supposed he had a point.

"We have to walk this way," she said, walking past the motel and heading toward downtown. "The path cuts off past the real-estate office."

"Speaking of real estate, I noticed your place is for sale."

Tabitha nodded, shoving her hands in her pockets, wishing she could act as casual as he seemed to be.

"So you're not rebuilding?"

A sudden flash of shame pierced her again as she thought of why that wouldn't happen. "No. I'm not. Don't have the energy."

She hurried down the sidewalk as if she was outrunning the memories, suddenly angry with him for making her go back to that humiliating moment in the insurance office.

"But you can hire someone to do it. The insurance would pay for it."

"Yeah, well, that's where things fall apart. I can't get the insurance company to pay for it because apparently they won't cover me because I had a woodstove in the house and I didn't know that."

"What? Why didn't you know that?"

"Because I didn't read the policy. And you know

why I didn't." She kept looking ahead, not wanting to see his face.

"The agent didn't read it to you?"

Tabitha walked past the office to a path leading to a trail along the river. "I was too ashamed to ask for her help," she murmured. "I assumed I was getting the same policy my dad had."

Morgan said nothing, and she was thankful. She didn't want to be faced, once again, with her shortcomings.

You are worth more than many sparrows.

The words resonated through her, and once again, she clung to them.

"So what does this mean?" Morgan asked.

Tabitha clenched her fists, fighting down the shame as her feet beat out a steady rhythm on the packed path. They were walking past trees now. The air was cool on her heated face. "If I can't rebuild the house, then all I have left is the land to sell. Which means less money to pay your father back."

"Is that why you stayed away from me? Because you can't pay my dad as much money as you hoped?"

He caught her by the arm and turned her toward him. She wanted to resist but was tired of fighting.

"Yes."

"I told you—it doesn't matter to him."

"Well, it does to me."

"And the first time you broke up with me? Why did you run away then?"

"I don't think we need to talk about that," she said.

"I think we do. Because when you didn't answer my phone calls the past few days, I thought it was a repeat of the first time. I was scared that you had decided you didn't want me. Again. I want to make a life with you but I can't keep thinking you're going to leave me whenever things get tough. So this time I'm not letting you walk away without telling me everything. I want to trust you but you need to show me I can. So, why did you leave me the first time?"

She held his gaze, still weighing. Still measuring.

"Why?" he insisted.

"I didn't want to tell you because I know how much you loved your mother and—"

"My mother? What does she have to do with it?" His defensiveness was almost her undoing.

In that moment, however, she knew she had to fight for him. For them. She had given in too easily before. He had come all the way here needing answers.

They came to a bench overlooking the river and she sat down, looking at the flowing water, letting it soothe her as she thought of what to tell him.

"After I quit school, your mother came to visit me to talk about me and you. Unfortunately she came to my dad's place. My place," she amended, mentally slipping back to that horrible time in her life. She faltered, but then pushed on, struggling to find the right words. "I had just come back from working with the horses and was dirty and grimy, and your mother, as she always did, looked so elegant. She told me we needed to talk about our relationship, yours and mine."

"My mother came to visit you?"

"Yes. She did."

She hesitated again, those humiliating words coming back. Haunting her.

Out of the corner of her eye she could see him watching her, eyes narrowed.

"What did she tell you?"

"She told me she had one message to deliver and one only. She wanted me to end our relationship. Somehow she had heard that you wanted to marry me and not go to veterinary school. She said she wasn't letting that happen."

"How did she hope to stop that?"

"By convincing me to break up with you. She said you were smart and had a bright future ahead of you. Then she reminded me that if I loved you, I wouldn't allow you to make that sacrifice. Her coup de grâce was when she told me that I wasn't worthy of you."

"And you believed her?"

She sighed. "Of course I did. I had quit school and was already struggling with a sense of self-worth. I knew what you were giving up to marry me and was feeling guilty over that. I still saw myself as the dumb girl. The one who wasn't good enough for a man like you. A man who had a bright future."

She could see Morgan's struggle to reconcile what she was saying with what he knew about his mother. Once again self-doubt assailed her.

"I know it's hard to believe this about your mother but it's what happened. I know you won't believe me." She was about to get up when she felt Morgan's hand on her arm, pulling her back. Once again he turned her to face him, his hand gently urging her to look at him.

"No. I want to believe you."

"Only want to?"

Morgan pulled in a long breath. "Hey, you toss this out at me and I'm supposed to just take it without questions?"

She wasn't sure what to think.

"Give me some credit here," he said, his voice holding a hint of pain. "This is new to me. I have to think about this. Let it sink in."

"Well, I have thought about it enough."

She got up and started walking away. She had finally told him the truth. Now it was up to him.

Morgan watched her go, struggling with what she had just told him. His mother? Chasing Tabitha away? Making her feel like she wasn't important?

And what am I doing now, just sitting here?

Morgan pushed aside his own doubts and ran after her. Like Leanne had told him to.

"Tabitha, wait," he said, catching her by the arm. Turning her to face him. "I'm sorry. I…I believe you."

Tabitha held his gaze as if testing his sincerity.

"I do. I know you don't lie. Why would you?"

"I know you cared about your mother—"

"Of course I did. She was my mother." He released a slow, melancholy smile. "But I also knew my mother wasn't crazy about you. She told me many times I should end our relationship. I never told you that because I thought she would come around and see you the way I saw you. I had no idea she had come to you directly. She never said anything to me. In fact, when I told her you had left, she said it was for the best. That if you couldn't stick with me, then maybe I was better off without you. I sensed she was wrong but I was too afraid to stand up to her. So I went along with what she said. That was wrong of me. I should have run after you. Taken that risk you said I was afraid to take."

Tabitha just looked at him, her arm tense beneath his

hand. Then she seemed to relax as his hand slipped to her shoulder, caressing it lightly.

"I couldn't tell you because I didn't want to come between you and your mother," she said. "Particularly when I thought she was right."

Morgan's eyes narrowed as a flash of anger surged through him. "You are an amazing person who has had a lot to deal with in her life. And I'm sorry for what my mother put you through. Put *us* through. But she was very, very wrong." He fought down a sense of loss and frustration with his mother. He tried to figure out what to do with the information Tabitha had just given him. "I wish you would have told me."

"How?"

Her simple question underlined the reality of his relationship with his mother. He thought back to what his father said. How his mother had spoiled him and Amber.

"Your mother was a teacher and I was a high school dropout," she continued. "Like I said, I thought she was right."

"And like *I* said, she wasn't."

"I know that now, but at the time I had many reasons to believe her."

"Do you now?"

She was quiet a moment, then slowly shook her head. "No. I know that God values me and that my worth is not in the stuff I have. I'll still struggle with it, but I hope I'm in a better place."

"With me too?"

"Especially with you."

"We've lost so many years…" His voice trailed off as sorrow replaced his anger.

Tabitha squeezed his hands, smiling at him. "But we're here now and, I'd like to think, stronger for what we've had to deal with. I know I've had to learn a few lessons. In realizing that God values me above many things, and that I only need His approval. Not your mother's. Not the community's."

He watched her, pride and admiration replacing the hollow anger he felt.

"I'm sorry I let you go back then," he said, his thumb stroking over her cheek. "I'm sorry I let you go without a fight. Yeah, it's hard to hear what you said about my mother, but in a way, it makes everything easier to understand."

She held his gaze, her eyes growing soft.

"I'm sorry" was all she said.

"You have nothing to apologize for. Nothing. You've been amazing through all this. A true example of strength and integrity that I, among many people, can learn from."

He leaned in and kissed her. Then he drew away from her, resting his forehead against hers.

"Tabitha, I'm never letting you get away from me again. I love you. Even more than I did when I wanted to marry you the first time."

She gave him a tremulous smile, then brushed a kiss over his lips. "I love you too."

"I'd like to try again," he said, digging into the pocket of his jeans and pulling out the same ring he had bought her all those years ago.

"Tabitha Rennie, will you marry me?"

Tabitha covered her mouth with her hands, her eyes shining. Then she threw her arms around him and hugged him tight. "Yes. I will. Of course I will."

She pulled back and he took her hand, slipping the ring on her finger, the diamond winking in the sunlight like a promise. He laughed. "It doesn't seem as big as I thought. It's the same one I had bought when I didn't make as much money—"

"It's perfect," she said, cutting him off. Then giving him another kiss. "Absolutely perfect." She held her hand up to look at it again.

Morgan felt as if he'd been running a marathon and could finally rest. He sat back on the bench and pulled her close, tucking her head under his chin. "I guess this is where we get to make plans."

Tabitha was quiet and Morgan felt a niggle of unease at her silence.

"Of course, we can wait—"

"No. I'm sorry. Plans are good," she said, fingering the button on his shirt. "It's just that I had such different ones. I'm not sure what to do about them now."

"You're thinking of your land."

She nodded, silent again.

Morgan drew in a slow breath, knowing that in spite of what he knew his father would say, Tabitha needed to finish this last piece of business.

"At any rate, we need to go tell my father and Nathan our good news. So when we do that, we can talk about the land and your debt. And assure Nathan that you aren't going to be out of his life." He hesitated to say the words but he knew that was how Tabitha saw it.

"Sure. Let's do that."

Frustration dampened the beauty of a moment so long in coming. But he also realized that if they dealt with this final issue, they could look to a future without shadows.

Chapter Seventeen

"Last chance," Morgan said. "You sure you want to do this now?"

Morgan turned to Tabitha, his arm resting on the steering wheel of his truck. They were parked in front of Boyce's house on a tree-lined street in Cedar Ridge. Morgan had called ahead and explained to Boyce that they would be coming and to please keep Nathan occupied. They needed to talk.

Boyce was curious but, thankfully, said nothing, only that he'd put on a television show for Nathan to watch so they could talk in peace.

Tabitha bit her lip, glancing from the diamond ring on her finger to the concern etched on Morgan's face.

She would have preferred to wait and enjoy the reality of her and Morgan, finally together.

But she also knew that, until she talked to Boyce, this would hang over their future.

"I'm sure."

"Okay. Let's do this."

They got out and walked hand in hand up the sidewalk to the house.

But then Morgan's father was at the door, holding it open, smiling as he looked from one to the other. "Come in," he said, stepping aside, his grin growing as he caught a glimpse of Tabitha's left hand. "I'm guessing you two have something good to tell me. Nathan is upstairs. He's watching television in my room. He doesn't know you're here. If he did, he wouldn't leave you alone, and I thought we might like some privacy."

That set Tabitha back. Clearly he knew exactly what they were here for.

They stepped into the house and Boyce limped ahead of them, leading them through the narrow hallway into the kitchen at the back. "I'll make some coffee."

"Don't bother, Dad," Morgan said. "We just want to talk with you."

"And talking is done best over a cup of coffee." Boyce shot Tabitha a smile. "You should know that, Tabitha. All those old guys yapping in the corner of the café in the morning when you used to work there."

Tabitha's smile felt forced as she settled into the old wooden chair at the small table. She sent up a prayer for strength, courage and hope.

A few awkward moments later, Boyce set down mugs in front of each of them and poured the coffee. Then he sat down himself, grinning. "So? What do you need to talk about?"

"I think you know that I've asked Tabitha to marry me and she's accepted," Morgan put in.

Boyce grinned. "I guessed that when I saw that ring on Tabitha's finger. Congratulations." He got up and gave Morgan a hug, then pulled Tabitha to her feet and held her close. "I'm so happy. Welcome to the family, my dear girl. I don't know if I should congratulate you or feel sorry for you."

Tabitha returned his hug, allowing herself a flicker of joy. It had been a long time since she'd received a hug from someone other than Morgan. "I'll take the congratulations but not the sympathy. I love your son. He's an amazing person."

Boyce patted Morgan on the shoulder. "I'd have to agree with you."

"But there's something else I need to talk to you about," Tabitha said, slowly sitting down, staying on the edge of her chair, her heart beginning a slow, heavy pounding. Morgan found her hand under the table and squeezed it, encouraging her. "And that's why we're here."

"You come to ask who's paying for the wedding? Well, that would be me, of course," Boyce said, grinning as he sat down as well. He took a sip of his coffee, looking from Morgan to Tabitha.

"No. Not that, though it does have to do with money." Tabitha bit her lip, hesitating, but then plunged on, needing to get this out of the way. "It has to do with the money my father stole from you."

Morgan's hand tightened and she shot him a grateful look, so thankful he was here beside her.

Boyce looked thoughtful as he turned his mug in circles, his silence making Tabitha even more on edge.

"Now, honey," he said slowly, drawing out his words. "I don't think you need to worry about that—"

"I know my father pulled a fast one when he shifted the title of my house—my former house—to me," she amended. "But I had every intention of making it right. That's why I was working so hard to fix it up. So that

I could make it worth more money. I wanted to sell it and pay you back. Pay off the debt my father owed."

Boyce's smile grew gentle and he leaned across the table. "Give me your hand, Tabitha. The one with that ring my son gave you."

Curious, Tabitha did as he asked. Boyce took hers in his rough, scarred and gnarled hands, his touch gentle as he touched the ring she wore. "See this ring? It means that you're going to marry my son. In my eyes, you saying yes makes you family. And family doesn't owe family money, so it all balances out."

His words almost made her cry.

"But my father isn't family—"

"And he's gone, God rest his soul. I don't know why he did what he did, but you shouldn't take that on," Boyce said, his eyes narrowing and his voice growing harsher. "You aren't your father and you aren't responsible for his wrongdoing."

"But it was so much money—"

"No. It was *only* money." Boyce leveled her a stern look. "Nothing more. Money isn't as important as people. That's something my daddy drilled into me and, I'm hoping, I instilled into my family." His expression grew softer and he was smiling again. "Like I said, it was only money. I got through it and so did everyone else. You're not responsible for what your father did."

Tabitha could only stare at him as his words registered.

"I know I love you and I know that God loves you," he continued. "That makes you valuable and that's all that matters. You also need to know that we all have bigger and more important debts that can't be paid. None of us righteous and none of us can stand before God with what we owe Him. He covered our debt. Covered yours. And that's a far more important debt than the one you seem to think you owe me. You are your own person, Tabitha Rennie. And you shouldn't let other people's mistakes or decisions determine how you see yourself. If God values you enough to send His son to save you, then you need to see your own value as well."

His words struck a chord. The same one she'd been hearing whenever she thought of the passage that stayed with her.

You are worth more than many sparrows.

But before she could react, Boyce slapped his hands on the table as if ending that particular line of thought. "And now, the only other financial thing we're going to talk about is what you were proposing to me, Morgan."

Tabitha struggled to wrap her head around what he was saying.

"Proposing? Other than marriage?" Tabitha asked, confused.

"I didn't have a chance to tell you, what with the proposal and all and hoping you would accept and then you wanting to clear things up with my dad," Morgan said, sounding breathless. "But I have a plan for that land of yours, if you're willing."

Tabitha shot Morgan a puzzled look. "What's that?"

"Well, I think it would be a great place for a new veterinary clinic. Your property is close enough to town and big enough that we could set up some pens and corrals and such."

"Wait, what? A vet clinic? What are you talking about?" She was struggling to keep up.

Morgan tucked a strand of hair behind her ear as he spoke. "I have this vet degree and the guy I'm working for doesn't give me enough hours and I know this amazing girl who has an equine health degree and acres of undeveloped land close to town that would be a perfect place for a clinic."

"A vet clinic? On my place?"

Morgan smiled. "I know it's all a bit much. I've only been here a few weeks but I can tell that things aren't going to get better with Dr. Waters. I had someone give me a pep talk recently on taking risks and I think I'm willing to do it. If I can advertise that I have an equine specialist who also trains horses, I would do that much better."

Tabitha shook her head, as if to process all this information.

"You should have waited to tell her like I told you to," Boyce said. "Now you're just confusing her."

"You're right. I'm jumping way ahead." Morgan brushed a light kiss over her forehead. "I'm excited to think about a future together." He pulled back and gave Tabitha a smile. "For now, why don't we focus on what we're telling Nathan."

"Tell him the straight-up facts," Boyce put in. "And from what I've seen of the boy, I think he'll be tickled pink."

Then he turned to Tabitha. "I'm so glad you and Morgan found each other again. I'm so glad you made it back here to Cedar Ridge and our family. You're family now."

Tabitha looked from Boyce to Morgan, the reality of what he said settling in. She was going to be part of a family.

She turned to Morgan. "Thank you for coming after me," she said.

"It took me a few years, but I can be taught." Then he kissed her again and got up from the table. "And now I'm going to get my son."

He left and Tabitha, still dazed, could only stare at Boyce, still trying to absorb everything that had happened, still not sure where to put it all.

"I'm happy for you," Boyce said, gifting her with a wide, cheerful grin. "I've always liked you and was sad when Morgan and you broke it off." He grew serious, frowning a little as he looked at his mug. "I know that my wife got between you two," he said, his voice growing quiet. "And I'm sorry for that."

"No, please... I don't want you to think—"

"I loved my wife but I also knew about her dreams for Morgan. They were good dreams but I also think she should have given you two a chance to plan your own life. There are many times I wish I had intervened. Said something to you, but you left and I didn't have a chance. I'm sorry for that."

His apology humbled her. "You have nothing to be sorry for," she said.

"And neither do you."

His words reinforced what he had said earlier and she slowly realized the truth of what he was saying.

Then a pair of footsteps came thundering down the stairs and Nathan burst into the room.

"Tabitha! You're here." He stopped in front of her, and then he frowned.

"Why did you leave?" His voice held an accusing tone that Tabitha knew she deserved.

"I had some things to sort out. I'm sorry," she said, hoping, praying he would forgive her. "But I'm back now."

Nathan walked over to Morgan, catching him by the hand, still frowning at her. The sight of him turning to his father warmed her heart even as his frown hurt her.

How would this little boy react to their news? Sure, he liked her, but that was as someone training his mother's horse. He had just got used to the idea that Morgan was in his life as his father. How would he react to her being his mother?

"Nathan, Tabitha and I have something to share with you," Morgan said, sitting down and taking Nathan's hand as if to prepare him. "I want you to know that I love Tabitha very much. And because we love each other, we want to get married."

Nathan frowned at that, glancing from Morgan to Tabitha. His confusion only increased Tabitha's apprehension.

"So does that mean you will be living in our house?" he asked, still sounding hesitant.

"After your father and I get married," Tabitha said, folding her hands on her lap, shooting Morgan a concerned look. He just smiled, then reached over, resting his hand on her shoulder.

Nathan seemed to consider this. Then a slow smile crept over his face. "So you'll be able to work with Stormy all the time then," he said.

"Tabitha will have work to do as well," Morgan said. "She'll be working with me when I start the new clinic."

"But when she lives with us, she can help teach me to ride after supper." Nathan's smile grew and Tabitha's worry shifted to a curious humor.

"I guess I could," she said.

"So does that mean you'll be my mommy?"

"It means I'll be helping to take care of you," Tabitha said, gently easing him into this new idea.

Nathan's grin grew and, to Tabitha's surprise, he threw his arms around her neck, giving her an awkward hug. Then he drew back and his expression grew serious. "I will still miss my other mommy," he said.

"Of course," Tabitha said, her hand tightening on his. "She'll always be your mommy. But I'm hoping that you will like having me around too."

"I really like you," he said, as if amazed she even questioned this. "We'll have fun together. We can ride horses and you can help Morgan...my dad make supper and you can tuck me in at night." He nodded with each statement as if underlining the reality of it. "It's all good."

Tabitha grinned at his succinct summary of the situation.

"I think it is too," she said, looking over his head at Morgan.

He returned her smile, then pulled closer, making the circle smaller, closer.

"I hope that we can be a blessing to each other," he said, his gaze holding hers, his love shining out of his eyes.

"I hope so too," she said.

Then, to her surprise, Morgan brushed a gentle kiss over her forehead. It was a whisper of his lips over her skin but it warmed her to her very soul.

"Well, this has been a long time coming," Boyce announced, getting up from his chair. "I can't wait to tell the crew at the Brand and Grill."

Morgan shot him a frown. "Maybe wait until we get a chance to tell a few people ourselves," he said.

"I guess so," Boyce said, pushing out a disappointed

sigh. "Anyhow, you let me know when I can pass on the news."

"We need to talk to Ella and Cord, which is where we are going next," Morgan said, getting up and pulling Tabitha to her feet. "Then find a way to let Amber know, wherever she is."

"I can't wait to go to Uncle Cord and Aunt Ella's place to tell Paul and Suzy," Nathan said, pulling away from them. "They will be so jealous that Tabitha is going to be my mommy." In his excitement he ran out of the house, slamming the door behind him.

"I better follow that boy," Boyce said, heading out the door of the kitchen that led outside.

Morgan chuckled as he pulled Tabitha close. "You don't mind telling the rest of my family right away?"

Tabitha shook her head. "I like the sound of that."

"What?"

"Family," Tabitha said, leaning into his hug.

"For better or worse, you're a part of all of this now." Morgan glanced at Tabitha, sharing a grin.

"Here's your last chance to change your mind," he said.

"Not a chance, Morgan Walsh. I let you go too easily the first time. There's no way I'm changing my mind now."

"You know I love you, Tabitha Rennie."

"I do. And I'm so thankful. And you know I love you."

"No doubts there."

She stood on tiptoe and brushed a kiss over his lips. "That's good. We've had enough of those in our past."

"So, let's go and face the future."

Tabitha slipped her arm around his waist and together they walked out the door to do exactly that.

* * * * *

If you loved this story,
check out COURTING THE COWBOY,
the first book in bestselling author Carolyne Aarsen's
miniseries COWBOYS OF CEDAR RIDGE,
and these other stories of love on the ranch
from Carolyne Aarsen

WRANGLING THE COWBOY'S HEART
TRUSTING THE COWBOY
THE COWBOY'S CHRISTMAS BABY

Available now from Love Inspired!
Find more great reads at www.LoveInspired.com

Dear Reader,

Tabitha struggled all her life with feelings of self-worth brought on by her father's actions and her own difficulty with reading. Both come together to create a situation where she feels she has to make up for what her father did in order to hold her head up. In the process of the story, she learns that her worth is in Christ, and not in doing things to fix what her father did.

I think there are times in each of our lives that we feel we have no value. No worth. It's not a good place to be because, as the Bible verse I quoted at the beginning of this book tells us, in God's eyes we are valuable and loved.

I pray that you may feel God's love and care and that you may place your worth in Him.

Carolyne Aarsen

P.S. I love to hear from my readers. Drop me a line at caarsen@xplornet.com and tell me what you liked about my book. Or you can go to my website at carolyneaarsen. com. If you sign up for my newsletter you'll get a free book.

COMING NEXT MONTH FROM
Love Inspired®

Available June 20, 2017

A SECRET AMISH LOVE
Women of Lancaster County • by Rebecca Kertz

With her father insisting she marry, Nell Stoltzfus is feeling the pressure to figure out her future. A decision that is further complicated when she falls for English veterinarian James Pierce. Dare she risk being shunned to be with the man her heart has claimed as its own?

THE COWBOY'S BABY BLESSING
Cowboy Country • by Deb Kastner

Cowboy Seth Howell's adventure-seeking days suddenly change when he inherits custody of his two-year-old godson. With day-care owner Rachel Perez by his side, teaching him how to care for little Caden, he'll learn that family is the greatest adventure of all.

HER COWBOY BOSS
The Prodigal Ranch • by Arlene James

Stark Burns and Meri Billings are like oil and water—so he's shocked when she asks for a position in his veterinary clinic. For Meri, it's her only option if she wants to stay close to home and family. Soon their differences fall away as Meri teaches the widower how to live—and love—again.

THE TWINS' FAMILY WISH
Wranglers Ranch • by Lois Richer

Finding someone to watch his orphaned twin niece and nephew is Rick Granger's priority—and he thinks teacher Penny Stern is just the person. Before long, he offers Penny a marriage of convenience for the children's sake—but will their pretend union turn into the future they both always wished for?

DEPUTY DADDY
Comfort Creek Lawmen • by Patricia Johns

Diaper duty was the last thing officer Bryce Camden expected during his stay in Comfort Creek. But with lovely Lily Ellison, owner of the B and B where he's staying, asking for his help with her foster baby, he'll soon be more than a bachelor cop—he'll be a family man.

CHILD WANTED
Willow's Haven • by Renee Andrews

Proven innocent of a crime she was unjustly accused of, Lindy Burnett desperately wants to regain her parental rights. Ethan Green is determined to adopt Lindy's son and protect him from harm. Can coming to an agreement about little Jerry also lead to an agreement to spend their lifetime together?

LOOK FOR THESE AND OTHER LOVE INSPIRED BOOKS WHEREVER BOOKS ARE SOLD, INCLUDING MOST BOOKSTORES, SUPERMARKETS, DISCOUNT STORES AND DRUGSTORES.

LICNM0617

SPECIAL EXCERPT FROM

*Nell Stoltzfus falls for the new local veterinarian in town,
James Pierce. But their love is forbidden since he's
English and she's Amish. If Nell follows her heart,
will love conquer all?*

Read on for a sneak preview of
A SECRET AMISH LOVE by **Rebecca Kertz**,
available July 2017 from Love Inspired!

"You said your *bruder* was called out on an emergency,"
Nell said. "What does he do?"

"He's a veterinarian. He's recently opened a clinic here
in Happiness."

The strange sensation settled over Nell. Despite the
difference in their last names, could James be Maggie's
brother? "What's his name?" she asked.

"James Pierce." Maggie smiled. "He owns Pierce
Veterinary Clinic. Have you heard of him?"

"*Ja.* In fact, 'twas your *bruder* who treated my dog,
Jonas."

"Then you've met him!" Maggie looked delighted. "Is he
a *gut* veterinarian?"

Startled by this new knowledge, Nell could only nod
at first. "He was wonderful with Jonas. He's a kind and
compassionate man." She studied Maggie and recognized
the family resemblance. "How is he a Pierce and you a
Troyer?"

"I am a Pierce." Maggie grinned. "Abigail is, too. But
we don't go by the Pierce name. Adam is our stepfather,

and he is our *dat* now." Maggie's eyes filled with sadness. "I was too young to care, but James had a hard time with it. He loved Dad, and he'd wanted to be a veterinarian like him since he was ten. He became more determined to follow in Dad's footsteps."

Nell felt her heart break for James, who must have suffered after his father's death. "You chose the Amish life, but James chose a different path."

"And he's doing well," Maggie said. "My family is thrilled that he set up his practice in Happiness."

Later that afternoon, James arrived to spend time with his family.

She recognized his car immediately as he drove into the barnyard. James stood a moment, searching for family members. Nell couldn't move as he crossed the yard to where tables and bench seats had been set up. Soon, James headed to the gathering of young people, including his sisters Maggie and Abigail.

Nell found it heartwarming to see that his siblings regarded him with the same depth of love and affection. James spoke briefly to Maggie, clearly delighted that he'd handled his emergency then decided to come. She heard the siblings teasing and the ensuing laughter. Maggie said something to James as she gestured in Nell's direction.

James saw her, and Nell froze. Her heart started to beat hard when he broke away from the group to approach her.

Don't miss
A SECRET AMISH LOVE
by Rebecca Kertz, available July 2017 wherever
Love Inspired® books and ebooks are sold.

www.LoveInspired.com